DECHIPPED: IRIS

THE UNCHIPPED SERIES
THE MEETING: AN UNCHIPPED SHORT STORY
UNCHIPPED: KAARINA
UNCHIPPED: WILLIAM
UNCHIPPED: ENYD
UNCHIPPED: LUNA
UNCHIPPED: THE RESORT
CHIPPED: LAURA
CHIPPED: DENNIS
CHIPPED: MARGARET
CHIPPED: JOVAN
CHIPPED: THE REVENANT
DECHIPPED: KRISTIAN
DECHIPPED: MARIA
DECHIPPED: OWENA
DECHIPPED: IRIS
DECHIPPED: THE DOWNLOAD
RECHIPPED: CITY OF SERBIA
RECHIPPED: CITY OF ENGLAND
RECHIPPED: CITY OF CALIFORNIA
RECHIPPED: CITY OF FINLAND
RECHIPPED: THE BUTTON

COMING SOON!
THE MACHINA DEUS SERIES (2024)
SERF GIRL
FAMA GIRL
SLUM GIRL

DECHIPPED: IRIS

TAYA DEVERE

CONTENT WARNING: SA, Predatory behavior. While not a main theme of the book, some readers may want to read the reviews or have a friend check out the book before reading.

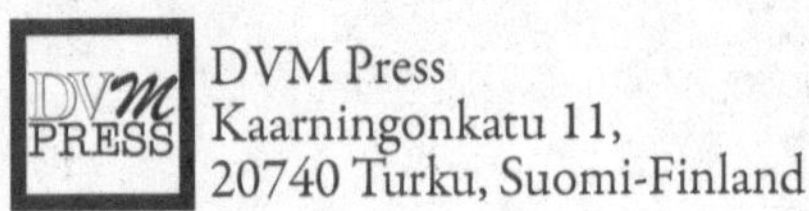
DVM Press
Kaarningonkatu 11,
20740 Turku, Suomi-Finland

www.dvmpress.com
www.tayadevere.com

For information about special discounts available for bulk purchases, sales promotions, fund-raising and educational needs, contact sales@dvmpress.com

ISBN 978-952-7404-41-6 First Ebook Edition
ISBN 978-952-7404-42-3 First Print Edition

Cover Design © 2021 by Deranged Doctor Design - www.derangeddoctordesign.com

Cover Spine Design © 2022 by Chris DeVere

Editing by Christopher Scott Thompson, Lindsay Fara Kaplan, and Elle Fort

To Jason.
In my books, your star will forever shine bright.

CONTENTS

SINKING

A short story in the world of the Unchipped series

Uploaded, The Egg, 2089

Her finger hovering above the video camera icon, Kaarina closes her eyes. Holding her breath, she wishes that Markus would say something to make her change her mind.

You mean you wish you *would say something*, she thinks, reminding herself that Markus doesn't exist in this new reality. It's just her. Kaarina, and her ever-growing need to learn what happened that day when her mother ended her life without a single word of goodbye.

This surreal state of her life is becoming impossible to bear. She tries to focus on the task at hand and keep her emotions in check. But the bitterness, the endless thoughts of why-the-hell-is-this-happening-to-me won't leave her be.

Markus is dead.

Because you ran out of the mansion.

Because of your stupidity. You are to blame.

You *are the reason he now exists only as a self-ish memory at the back of your rotting brain. Just a self-serving creation of your mind* . . .

Kaarina stops to stare into space as the realization hits her hard. *Just like your mother's empty note.* Because . . . there is no note. No hidden meaning. Just a worthless inkling—a hunch—of something not being right. Is it even worth chasing after, her foolish mind's desperate creation? What if it's just her need for her mother not to have abandoned her?

Painful thoughts and memories fill her mind. Kaarina slams her fist against the Home-Helper's monitor, but the impact doesn't break the screen as she wished it would. The IT room glitches around her as she gasps for air and tries to calm her raging mind.

"Are you okay?" Markus's ghost asks from somewhere nearby. "Is the AI not finding the security camera feed?"

"No, it did," Kaarina replies to the ghost, her voice shaking. "Or at least the last two hours of it."

"Is the screen frozen?"

Kaarina hangs her head. It takes all she has to take a deep breath, then exhale slowly. She needs to watch the footage. She needs to know why that note was blank; why she's so sure it was her mother's suicide note. Why she herself was abandoned. But most of all, she needs to know what happened that day in the house where she grew up.

"Maybe if you . . . "

"Markus, I got this. Just . . . " Kaarina curses the hostility in her voice. She's not being fair—only moments ago she was hoping Markus would intervene. "Just let me do this on my own. Okay?"

And just like that, Markus is gone. Kaarina's mind has hidden him somewhere, socked him away for future use. Or maybe she just recreates the man every time she needs him to hold her hand? Who knows how this place really works. Kaarina sure as hell doesn't.

She stands taller and takes a breath. The cold IT room flickers around her, but the walls settle down again once she succeeds in taking another deep inhale. And another.

"Miranda," she says to the AI. "Play the security feed."

PLAYING SECURITY FEED – SEPTEMBER 23, 2088

The sight of a familiar kitchen table appears on the Home-Helper's screen. Kaarina's mother sits at the end of the table, eating a piece of crispbread while her dog, Ässä, drools and pretends not to be begging next to her on the floor. The rest of the seats around the kitchen table are empty.

Kaarina muffles a sob and looks away. After a ragged breath, she slowly turns her gaze back to the screen. She taps the monitor twice to bring up the control buttons.

"Miranda, fast-forward one hour."

FAST-FORWARD OPTION – NOT AVAILABLE

"What do you mean not av . . . " Kaarina scoffs at the AI. "I said, skip forward one hour."

FAST-FORWARD OPTION – NOT AVAILABLE

"Oh, for fuck's sake . . . " Kaarina taps the monitor repeatedly. "This is *my* mind. You work for me. If I say you skip, you ask how far."

FAST-FORWARD OPTION – NOT AVAILABLE

The scream starts from somewhere at the back of her muddled and frantic mind. She screams so loudly she can nearly feel her dead and buried lungs burning as they empty of all air. Then she screams some more, grabbing onto the Home-Helper screen as if to rip the stupid piece of junk off the wall of her imagination and cast it down onto the floor of the Egg.

The walls start to shake. Suddenly, the air crackles with static. A prism of otherworldly blue rays pours from the crumbling walls.

She howls louder.

The ground underneath her pitches alarmingly. Kaarina stumbles backward, glancing around in confusion. Then her eyes lock on the Home-Helper's crackling monitor, where she sees her mother step into the bathroom and stare directly into the camera. She must have been looking at herself in the mirror, but since the camera is in the mirror it seems as if she's staring straight into Kaarina's eyes.

"Miranda, pause feed."

PAUSED SECURITY FEED – SEPTEMBER 23, 2088

The floor lurches, then rumbles underneath her. Kaarina loses her balance and tumbles into a gaping crack in the concrete floor. Oddly, Kaarina hears waves breaking, followed by a grinding reverberation. She shields her head with her arms and squeezes her eyes shut. She screams again—this time in fear.

After falling helplessly—sinking—for what could be seconds, minutes, or hours, Kaarina finally thumps against solid ground. Restless waves swarm around her, then gradually travel farther away. Soon, she no longer hears water surrounding her, but something else. Something more . . . solid. Swaying trees. Crackling ice floes. Hostile wind. Without opening her eyes, she feels the wind tossing powdered snow on her face. Murky skies crunch and crackle with a blanket of thunderous clouds above.

Bundled into herself and lying on the hard surface, Kaarina listens as her surroundings slowly scrunch together as if to take a new form. Once the sounds settle, fade, and then vanish altogether, she opens her eyes, her arms still wrapped protectively around her head. Ice. A thick layer of ice. That's all she sees, as she evens her breath and rapidly blinks her eyes.

"Ma . . . Markus?"

But the ghost is not there.

"Miranda?"

HOME-HELPER – ACTIVATED. The voice travels across the frozen seascape.

Snowflakes swirl downward around Kaarina, and though she can't feel the frost biting her face and body, she is now shivering. One hand at a time, she takes support from the hard surface and pushes herself up. Once she's sitting on her hindquarters, she stops to listen. Is the ice cracking under her weight? Slowly, she drops to her hands and knees, then moves her weight to her left hand to see if the ice holds. A small crack appears, darting out from under her palm, then traveling a few inches toward her feet. Kaarina inhales sharply and freezes in place. She sits back down, staring at the fractured ice.

"Miranda," she says. "Play the security tape."

PLAYING SECURITY FEED – SEPTEMBER 23, 2088

A blue light fills the sky above her, flickering and glowing like some cyber version of the northern lights. Soon, up in the sky that now shows the security feed like some giant, otherworldly cinema, Kaarina gazes into her mother's eyes, staring into a bathroom mirror and the hidden camera within. The sky fills with a *pop* as her mother opens the cap on the pill bottle she's holding. With her index finger and thumb, she fishes out a white pill, shaped like a tiny American football. She holds it up to the bathroom light, investigating it as if seeing medicine for the first time.

"What is that, Miranda?" Kaarina says and fidgets on her seat. She stumbles up to sit on her knees. The crack in the ice travels toward her, growing in length by multiple inches.

ANALYSIS – NOT AVAILABLE

Kaarina sits still, her hands gripping her knees, holding her breath. After staring at the ice for a while, she looks up at the sky again. Murky clouds move in, surrounding the blue glow—and her mother's face. The snow has turned into rain. Shivering, Kaarina forces a breath, then says, "Miranda, resume the security feed."

PLAYING SECURITY FEED – SEPTEMBER 23, 2088

After staring at the medicine in her hand, Kaarina's mother claps the pill into her mouth. A couple of steps take her from the sauna bench to the bathroom sink. She takes a gulp of water and washes the pill down. Leaning against the sink, she looks into the mirror, her bottle-green eyes once again staring at Kaarina.

Those are not suicidal eyes, Kaarina thinks and stares back. *Those are rebel eyes.*

Smiling, her mother turns to leave the bathroom. But as she reaches for the door handle, she suddenly hangs her head, then grasps it with both hands. Stumbling backward, she slumps onto the bathroom floor. Foam dripping from her mouth, she bundles into herself, her eyes locked on the mirror.

"Front door—unlocked." Miranda's voice on the security feed sounds like it's coming from under water. *"Test subject—vital signs low."*

"No..." Kaarina exhales. Tears should be streaming down her face, but the pain she feels stays bottled up inside her, with no release. "No, it can't be."

The bathroom door opens. A woman in a white doctor's coat and a pair of white lab shoes leans forward to inspect the cold, sweat-covered face of Kaarina's mother.

"You!" Kaarina leaps up, ignoring the rapidly cracking ice underneath her feet. "You sadistic..." she gasps for air, "murdering...psychopath."

Doctor Solomon kneels next to Kaarina's unmoving mother. She carefully places a pill bottle into her upturned palm. Kaarina recognizes the bottle with the red triangle on its side. It's the same one she found when she walked into that bathroom to discover her allegedly suicidal mother's body.

"That's why your suicide note was blank," Kaarina says. She clenches her fists tight. "You never killed yourself. Solomon did."

"So sorry about this, dear," Doctor Solomon says, scattering colorful pills around Kaarina's mother's motionless body. They spread around the white bathroom tiles, some landing in her hair, some rolling under the sauna bench a few feet away. "Should have kept your thoughts to yourself. People like you are simply too dangerous to keep around."

Kaarina's scream travels across the frozen ocean. Booming with echo, her scream grows stronger, climbing up the invisible walls of powdered snow and wind until it fills the restless and thunderous sky. After spreading in the gloomy clouds like a wildfire, hurricanes given life by her raging voice slam back down, swirling, drilling into the ice. Breaking the now rattling floes, it fills the whole ocean beneath. She stomps on the ice, fracturing the surface further. The widening cracks on the ice snake forward, forming little ice floes, slowly creaking apart from one another.

"You killed my mother!" Kaarina wails at the sky. She yells at the Egg, at Doctor Solomon, who's somewhere here with her. With Kaarina's friends. Her allies. Her Yeti. That sick, malicious piece of scum has taken everything from her—and lied about it since day one. She's not remorseful. She hasn't come to her senses because of her Unchipped daughter. Laura Solomon saved nobody that day in the burning mansion. Everything she has ever done, she has done to help and benefit one person, and one person only: Laura Solomon herself.

Kaarina's knees buckle, then give out. She falls hard against the ice. A cracking sound fills her ears, and she closes her eyes, ignoring her crumbling surroundings. Her chest heaves with sobs, but no tears appear on her face. The anger, bitterness, and hatred build up within. Kaarina punches the ice hard with her fist. It hurts her knuckles, but she hardly notices. She hits the ice again. Then with two hands. Once more.

The ice underneath her collapses. Falling into the water turns her stomach, but she doesn't try and struggle back up to the surface. As she sinks deeper, she looks up at her mother's lifeless face and the colorful pills surrounding her corpse.

The white coat slips away through the bathroom door like a ghost. Like someone who never existed. Someone who had nothing to do with Kaarina's mother's death. Miranda falls silent as well. Not a sound echoes in the bathroom. Dead and empty. That's all there is left—and the humming sound of the ocean as Kaarina descends toward her own nonexistence.

She closes her eyes.

She opens her fists.

She takes in two lungsful of water.

Then she waits.

A soothing calm washes over her as she becomes one with the water. It feels pleasant against her skin. The force that pulls her feet toward the bottom is reassuring. The bigger the growing distance between Kaarina and the one who murdered her family and then brainwashed her friends, the calmer she feels.

You win, she thinks as she relaxes her arms and lets them float above her head. Drowning. *Evil overcomes good. I lose. You win. So be it.*

The sound of rain drumming against the ice ceiling reaches her ears. The current around her gurgles steadily as the humming and swooshing of the water fills Kaarina's mind. When she opens her eyes to look up, all she sees is a distant blue glow.

Suddenly, three white dots appear above her head. They run across the glow of the sky, at the shrinking spot where the ice has broken and the ocean's surface slowly undulates.

OWENA BELL CALLING

Water muffles Miranda's robotic voice, but the words are still loud and clear in Kaarina's ears. She tugs hesitantly against the current that's pulling her under.

What the hell . . .

The three dots seem to plummet down and catch up with Kaarina as she drifts toward the ocean bed.

OWENA BELL CALLING

But I'm not wearing my AR-glasses, she thinks, unable to block these strange thoughts disturbing her peaceful drowning. *And of all people . . .* Owena *is calling me?*

OWENA BELL CALLING

"I heard you the first time!" Kaarina yells at Miranda. The water doesn't muffle her voice like it should. "I'm not going to answer a fucking AR-call while I'm drowning myself!"

ANSWERING CALL

"That's not what I . . ." Kaarina groans in frustration. She extends her arms at her sides, and the movement stops her from falling deeper into the ocean's throat. As she floats in the darkening water, she looks up at the hole in the ice, then listens carefully. Not a peep sounds from above.

"Owena?" she whispers.

Someone clears their throat on the line. How is this possible? Is her mind playing tricks on her? Has Markus found a way to call her through the Home-Helper? Markus . . . being her own mind? Is she saving herself from her own suicide attempt?

She holds her head, then taps herself on her temples repeatedly. It's hard to focus. The line between what's possible and what is not is blurring and fading away minute by minute. Of course people can call her—she's inside a computer system. And why is she so afraid of drowning? Dying? After all . . . she's already dead.

"Kaarina Aho?" an unmuffled, nasal voice asks, snapping Kaarina out of her muddled but racing thoughts.

Kaarina holds her breath, then kicks her legs a few times to swim a bit closer to the sound above. "This, um . . . " She shakes her head, then kicks a few times more. "This is she."

"Ah, good. This is Nurse Saarinen calling. But you probably knew that already."

"Can't say that I did."

"Oh."

"It said Owena Bell." Kaarina waves her arms and swims a meter closer to the ice ceiling. "Is she . . . Is Owena okay?"

"I wouldn't know," Nurse Saarinen says with her matter-of-fact voice. "She's no longer with me. This call is just forwarded through her AR-glasses."

"Why?"

Kaarina can almost hear Nurse Saarinen shrugging. "She owes me a favor."

A few more kicks and waves of her arms, and Kaarina is so close to the surface that all she needs to do is reach for the ice, and she could pull herself back up onto the ground. The brisk wind has pushed away the murky clouds, changing the sky's hue from indigo to piercing white.

White coat.

White shoes.

White pill.

Kaarina stops kicking and lets herself float slowly downward again. She closes her eyes when the images of her mother's lifeless face rush in.

"She murdered my mother . . ." she whispers.

"What's that?" the nasal voice asks with a hint of surprise.

"Solomon. She gave my mother a pill. Must have lied about what it would do to her. My mother never left me. She was taken from me."

For a moment, the line stays quiet. Kaarina floats in the water, not sinking but not kicking for the surface either.

"I see." Nurse Saarinen clears her throat. "And who told you this?"

"Miranda."

"Who?"

"My mother's Home-Helper."

"Aha." Nurse Saarinen seems to hesitate with her words. "And what else did you learn about your mother's last moments?"

"Only the last two hours or so. The security feed wouldn't rewind or forward."

"I see," Nurse Saarinen repeats, a hint of satisfaction or relief in her voice. "Well, Laura is known to dispense with those who question her vision. Unfortunately, your mother was such a person. Maija was quite pleasant. I remember her well."

"You do?"

"Yes. We worked together for years at the hospital, until The Great Affliction."

Kaarina wiggles her feet, then circles her hands to move toward the ice ceiling. She doesn't care if Nurse Saarinen worked with her mother. Whether she thinks she was a good person or not. All Kaarina really cares about is . . .

"I want her to pay."

"And who is that?" Nurse Saarinen asks slowly. "Laura?"

"Yes." Kaarina kicks hard with her legs and takes a few strokes to reach the hole in the ice. She floats just beneath the surface, then pulls herself back up. Soaking wet, she isn't shivering. Focused is all she feels. The hatred she feels now more than ever before presses against her chest, then travels up her throat, finally fills her whole being. "I want her to suffer."

"Well . . . " Nurse Saarinen's tone of voice warms with pleasure. This time, instead of a shrug, Kaarina can sense a smug smile take over her face. "It just so happens . . . that's why I'm calling."

14
IRIS

December 2089
City of England

CHAPTER 1
TEA FOR THE DECHIPPED

Her steps slow as she nears the punching bag. Feet shoulder-distance apart and staggered with one foot in front of the other, Iris narrows her eyes and imagines the bag to be flesh and bones—filled with ill intentions. A sack of filth wrapped in the shape of a man.

She raises her hands, positions them like she's prepared to punch. She throws two punches in quick succession, first jabbing with her left arm, then crossing with her right. After a quick duck, she repeats the jab-cross-squat sequence. Lost in flow, she skips the squats, punching the bag with all she has. Left, right. Left, right. Dripping sweat, tears burning her squinting eyes, Iris stares at the sack of meat, imagining a face she only allows herself to remember when she's training.

Jab-cross. Jab-cross. Out of breath, completely focused, Iris nearly misses the gym door clicking open behind her. Soft steps across the floor don't interrupt her perfect focus. She squats down, jumps right back up again, and punches the bag with more force.

Her forearms are burning. Tears fill her narrowed eyes, but Iris doesn't stop. Not even when the old woman circles the punching bag and stands quietly at a safe distance.

Jab-cross-knee.

Jab-cross-round.

Jab-rear hook-front hook.

Hook-hook-upper-upper.

Front-kick-jab-cross.

Jab-cross-jab-knee.

Her thighs go numb. It's only been a few hours since Iris last visited the gym—for this very reason. Obsessive or not, it's better this way. No matter how many times the doctors tell her to refrain from exercise for seven to ten days after her dechipping operation.

Jab-jab-cross-cross-squat.

"How about a break, dear?"

Jab-jab-jab. Iris shuffles and moves around the punching bag. The old woman, holding something steaming in her hands, now stands behind her back.

"I'm not telling you to stop . . . "

Jab-cross. Jab-cross.

"But I made tea. Icelandic moss."

A quick squat down leaves Iris kneeling on the floor. Out of breath, her legs numb and powerless, she pants, wiping her forehead on the back of her arm. She doesn't answer Mrs. Salonen or glance up to send a nasty look in her general direction.

Leave me the fuck alone, she thinks, but bites her tongue. It's only been a few hours since she last tortured her body with an extended kickboxing session, and it's only been two hours since Iris last snapped and yelled at the woman—for interrupting her practice to tell her the sauna was heated and ready.

She hears Mrs. Salonen approach her with careful steps. Iris leans back and sits on the floor with her legs spread, tossing her head back to move the blue and white lock of hair off her face. When Mrs. Salonen kneels down and sits in front of her, Iris doesn't tell her to leave. After placing a tray with two steaming mugs of tea between them, Mrs. Salonen winces and tries to find a better position on the hard floor. For a woman her age—and with her iffy hip—the gym's cold floor is the last place she should sit for a cup of tea. Guilt nags at Iris, but with a quick shake of her head, she refuses to listen to it.

She never invited Mrs. Salonen to come here. *Just like I didn't ask her to make me moss fucking tea.*

Her eyes soft and friendly, Mrs. Salonen brings her tea close to her face, then blows into the mug, supporting her hip with her free arm. "Laura was asking about you today," she says matter-of-factly. "It's been a while since the two of you talked."

"Yeah, well," Iris says with a scoff, staring at her mug on the floor. Instead of reaching for the moss tea, she looks around to find her sports drink bottle, but she must have forgotten to bring it from the locker room. "Speaking with the dead isn't really my cup of . . . tea." She gives Mrs. Salonen a quick look but doesn't return her amused smile. "Pun not intended."

"Laura had some news," the old woman says, her voice more careful than before. "It's about Iceland."

A sharp, cutting pain passes through Iris's stomach, but she doesn't let on. She's stronger than that—with or without a chip in her brain. Revealing pain is a vulnerability. A soft spot. Being vulnerable is the biggest no-no. If Laura Solomon taught Iris anything, that would be it. "Let me guess," she says. "Nurse Saarinen finally pulled the trigger. Or pushed a button. Whatever."

Mrs. Salonen nods. "I'm afraid so."

"It's all gone?" Iris says, staring over the old woman's shoulder, focusing on fighting the burning sensation at the back of her eyes. "The resort. The village. The barns. All of it?"

Just like my chip, she thinks but doesn't say that part aloud. *The only thing that made me special. Worthy of Laura's attention.*

After a small sigh, Mrs. Salonen pauses and focuses on stirring her tea. Again, she blows into the cup carefully, places her palm on top of the steam, then lowers the cup back down to the floor. "How's your head, dear?"

"Still fucking attached."

A small twitch at the corner of the old woman's lips tells Iris what she already knows; she isn't bothered by Iris's angst. "I understand," Mrs. Salonen says, tilting her head in a motherly way. "It is *such* a big change. You need time to adjust."

"I don't need shit. I told you, I'll deal with the storage pods. I'll integrate the ICE test subjects with their new fucking coffins."

Iris swallows as mental images of stasis capsules and white long-storage pods flash through her mind's eye. Staring at the elevator door is the closest she's gotten to working on organizing the massive pod farm downstairs.

"I see," Mrs. Salonen says. She tilts her head to the other side. "And when is this happening?"

"Tomorrow."

"Ah," Mrs. Salonen says, her lip twitching as she takes a careful sip of her tea. "Tomorrow it is, then."

"And what is that supposed to mean?"

"What, dear?"

Iris narrows her eyes at the old woman. "You're not even going to bitch at me . . . are you?"

The woman shakes her head. With a small smile, she reaches for her mug on the floor. "If you say you'll come back to work tomorrow . . ." She pauses for a careful sip of tea. "Tomorrow it is."

"Whatever."

Iris has been telling Mrs. Salonen she'd deal with what awaits downstairs "tomorrow" for what must be seven or eight weeks now, ever since the shipment of stasis capsules from Iceland arrived. All along, they knew Nurse Saarinen would destroy the resort in Iceland. Grudgingly, Iris had finally agreed to pack her few belongings, gather the resort's animals for transport, and leave her home country with Mrs. Salonen to relocate to a safer place—City of England—where they'd continue the fight against Nurse Saarinen and the Happiness-Program.

But the thought of doing the work without being chipped is nauseating. Every time Iris walks to the elevator to travel down to the basement, her world starts spinning. Her breath becomes shallow. A tinny sound takes over her ears. For the first time in years, she feels weak again. So she keeps turning around, heading back to the gym or the Chip-Center's roof to gasp for fresh air.

After burning her tongue when going for a sip of tea, Iris sets the mug on the floor and stands up hastily. The room spins around her, forcing her to freeze and rebalance. Once her brain adjusts after the sudden movement, she steps away from Mrs. Salonen and turns her back on her, facing the bag. As Iris lands the first punch, she hears Mrs. Salonen arranging the tea mugs on the tray, then struggling up from the floor. Iris wonders if the old woman secretly wishes that her stasis capsule's healing properties would have been turned on, back when Iris and Laura cornered her and shoved her in her Icelandic prison years ago. But somehow, Iris knows healing and improving Mrs. Salonen while storing her away would have made her even more upset. It's bad enough that her own daughter shoved her in a capsule, at least Laura had honored her mother's wishes against being rejuvenated. Keeping her gaze on the bag's torn leather, Iris tries to ignore the woman as she walks over and sets something on the floor next to Iris.

"I'll see you tomorrow, dear."

Soon, a loud click fills the room as Mrs. Salonen closes the gym door behind her.

Jab-jab-cross-cross-squat.

Iris shakes her head, trying to lose the image of endless rows of smooth-surfaced pod capsules bathe in an eerie red light. Millions and millions of people, forgotten, turned off, abandoned, underneath City of England. Research labs and storage spaces are all that is left of City of England today. Though Nurse Saarinen is in charge of it all, she has no idea that Mrs. Salonen and Iris have taken over the Chip-Center, quietly doing research of their own. Saarinen now seems to operate exclusively from her bunker in City of Spain, hiding in plain sight, leaving places like City of England abandoned and out of use.

Jab-cross-squat.

When Iris tries to come back up from her squat, her legs give out. She falls on her ass on the floor, then lets her upper body go limp. Chest heaving, she moves into a fetal position and rests her hollow-feeling head against her arm. Iris's face feels hot as the agitation washes over her body.

Why is the old woman so good to me? Why can't she just scream at me? Tell me what a piece of shit I am?

She should spit in Iris's face. She should lock her away in one of the glass boxes down in the labs. Tase her. Slap her. She should send her to the United Inland, abandon her to survive on her own.

But no. No, no, no. Not Mrs. Salonen. Her softness and understanding are a trigger for Iris, though she's unsure why. It makes her want to scream. Kick. Stab. Not everyone deserves a second chance. Some people should be stored away in one of those hell-pods, without a release date.

People like Iris.

She gets up from the floor, her thighs numb and calves threateningly wobbly. She brushes her shredded knuckles against the bag. Still slightly out of breath, she leans in and wraps her arm around it, balancing herself against the bag's shaky support. Like a lousy parent, the bag keeps Iris standing, but just barely. Any moment now, she could fall. Any moment now, the bag could snap from the hook on the ceiling, come crashing down on Iris. Any moment now, this false security the bag is giving her could disappear, kicking her legs out from underneath her.

Let it, she thinks. *What else is new?*

It wouldn't be the first time that something that was supposed to support and protect her turned against Iris and ruined her soul.

CHAPTER 2
THE ALGORITHM
(5 YEARS EARLIER)

"Let go of the inside rein!" The sound of his agitated voice fills the enormous indoor arena. Her own intermittent breath in her ears, Iris moves her right hand forward toward the horse's wither. She activates her lower stomach muscles, trying to find movement within the horse's movement.

"You're doing it again!" the man yells from the corner of the riding arena. "Let go," he pauses for emphasis, "of the *fucking* rein!"

Sweat drips from under Iris's riding helmet. It's minus twenty Celsius outside, but riding in the indoor arena feels like a swim in one of the hot water springs surrounding this barn she lives and works in.

"Okay, stop. Stop, stop, stop."

Iris bears down on her seat and closes her fists on the reins. The gelding stops, his nostrils puffing and his neck foaming. Just like Iris, the horse has been going on fumes for the last thirty minutes—when the training session should have ended but didn't. She reaches for the gelding's withers and scratches slightly, then pulls her hand quickly away, cursing her mistake in her mind.

Her trainer's shiny dressage boots freeze a few meters away on the sand and rubber arena floor. Although Iris doesn't look over to see Timothy Walker's wrathful face, she knows his eyes are locked on Iris's left hand.

"Pat . . . " he pauses to give Iris a brief, dry laugh. "You *patted* him? What in the world makes you think he needs to be rewarded right now?"

"Sorry, Mister Walker." Iris closes her eyes and looks away, again cursing at herself.

"And who the *fuck* said you could talk back at me? How many *trillion* times do I need to tell you before you get it through your monkey brain? You. Do. Not. Talk. You sit up there, keep your ass and private parts glued to the saddle, and shut. The fuck. *Up*. Is that understood?"

Iris holds her breath and gives a small nod. The words spat out by her world-famous trainer echo in the empty arena. It's six-thirty in the morning. Though the horses are all fed and resting in their run-out paddocks, no other riders are present. Tina's still sound asleep. It's just Tim and Iris. And the poor gelding, Romeo, trying to get his breathing under control.

When the fuming man steps closer, Romeo lifts his neck, flashing the white of his eye. His whole seven hundred kilo body goes rigid under Iris's seat.

"Honestly," Tim breathes out and crosses his long, slim arms on his chest. "You'll be eighteen in, what, six fucking days? If you want to make it to the big girl's league, I need you to start taking this seriously. None of this . . . " he circles his hand in the air frantically, "this shit-show. Can't you see your horse is struggling? You sit up there, trying to look all cute and pretty, when in reality you look like a monkey on a fucking stick. Feet sticking out, your hands doing . . . " He pauses to scoff. "I honestly don't know *what* is up with your fucking hands, but your head bobs around like the empty bucket it is. You think I want to be here at six in the morning, watching this . . . this . . . *joke*? Do you?"

Iris shakes her head once. Her cheeks burn, but she's unsure whether it's because of physical exhaustion, anger, or embarrassment. Probably a little bit of each.

"That's right. I don't. You think I wanted to leave the states and move up here to freeze my balls and watch some mediocre rider hump a mediocre horse day in and day out?"

Iris gasps for air, holds it, and fights the urge to let her mind travel somewhere else, on a mental vessel she created a long, long time ago. Well before Timothy Walker ever set foot in her home country of Iceland.

He spreads his hands, then lets them fall at his side. A loud *slap* sound fills the indoor arena. Romeo tenses under Iris but stays put, his head turned slightly away from the man next to him. Iris's hand twitches to scratch the gelding's neck, but she catches herself before she makes the same mistake twice in a row.

Tim turns around, heading back to his red trainer's chair in the corner of the arena. Before he sits down, he reaches for a dressage whip, then lifts it above his head and circles it around once. "One more time," his voice booms in the hall. "And get it fucking done this time." What follows is just a murmur, but loud enough for Iris to hear as she picks up the right lead counter canter precisely in the middle of the short side. "Don't make me send your ass back to whatever igloo or ice hole you first crawled out of."

The numbers run across the computer screen. Her feet throbbing in pain, Iris moves her hips to find a more comfortable position on the hard mattress. The wind blows outside, sending a freezing cold draft across the bedroom. Iris glances at the radiator longingly, then drops her chin in defeat. If she wanted a warmer room, she'd need to pay Timothy for heat. But because all her money goes into training, she can barely make her rent. So the heat from the barn downstairs, where the horses munch their nightly hay, will have to do.

Sighing, she gets up and heads to the small closet by the door. When she opens the closet door and reaches for the extra blanket, a barn spider takes off and disappears into the crack at the back of the upper shelf.

Two fleece blankets wrapped around her aching body, Iris sits back on her bed and reaches for the laptop. The green code keeps running, numbers and letters taking on a life of their own. Hacking into databases is soothing. Overwhelmed by her day at the barn, Iris hasn't been able to fall asleep after tossing and turning for an hour. She fires up her computer—as she has so many times before—and dives into a world where Timothy Walker has no place.

But he does, Iris reminds herself. *This is exactly the world the great Mister Walker rules.*

She opens another tab and refreshes the website.

DRESSAGE WORLD CUP 2084

She browses the site, clicking on headings.

COUNTRIES PARTICIPATING

RIDERS – TO BE CONFIRMED

TRAINERS – LISTED IN ALPHABETICAL ORDER

As she has many times before, Iris scrolls down to the end of the trainers' list.

MISTER TIMOTHY WALKER (USA/ICELAND)

Never in a million years had she thought to find herself in this position; working and training for the one and only Mister Walker. Iris is shortlisted for the last World Cup of dressage. It's between her and Timothy's other working student, Tina. Though both of the girls are anxious for the trainer to make it official and announce which of them will ride at the Cup, all signs point toward Tina. But Iris hasn't given up. She just has to prove herself.

Show off.

Work harder.

Become more visible, louder—impossible to ignore.

If Tim's home country, the United States, wasn't in such turmoil, he would never have ended up here in Iceland. After the mass murders ravaged most of the great American cities, the phenomena people now call The Great Affliction has made dressage along with other great sports a thing of the past.

Iceland is the only place in Europe where unrest, death, and violence haven't taken place at all. It's no wonder the American Dressage Society turned its hopeful gaze to Iris's nearly deserted northern home. Timothy isn't the only American trainer to pack his bags and horses and move up north. But as far as Iris knows, it didn't take the other barns long to close their doors and give up.

Iceland isn't without its own problems; births have been few and far between for decades. Older, retired people hardly had anyone to take care of them as the government slowly shut down. More and more of the nation was forced to participate in the relocation program moving people to live in compounds in central Europe. Tourism is now just a distant memory. Even in the one resort left open for business, the incoming buses are canceled more often than not, or else they simply arrive at the hotel empty.

But it is peaceful. No mass murders. No riots. Nothing.

A *cling* sound from the laptop startles Iris and pulls her back to this moment. She switches tabs and leans closer to the screen. The computer she's hacked into is located in the Netherlands.

"In-house trainer Mila Van Dijk . . . " Iris mumbles as her gaze scans the backend information that is not meant for her eyes. The server and database belong to the record-holding dressage facility Van Dijk Sport Horses. Though the unrest has interrupted most of the dressage business in Netherlands' provinces, one of them is still thriving—Friesland. Out of the five countries participating in the World Cup—Iceland, Netherlands, Sweden, France, and Germany—Netherlands has been the winner for the last five years.

"Huh . . ." Iris breathes out as she dives deeper into Van Dijk's database. "What's this, an algorithm?"

For the next four hours, Iris studies the numbers. She memorizes all she can, learning how her trainer's opponent uses AI to analyze each rider, horse, and training session, finding the ultimate combination to participate in the World Cup. Her mind takes over, numbing down all her body's aches, her fatigue, her self-doubt.

The alarm clock startles her, making her jump up from the bed. Four o'clock.

"Fuck . . ."

She's spent the whole night reading the code. Learning what makes the perfect rider, the perfect horse, and the perfect combination of the two. Could this be it? Her ticket to success?

Two fleece blankets fall onto the floor. Iris pulls on her breeches and ties her white-blue hair in a tight ponytail. Without a bite to eat, she takes the stairs down to the barn and starts piling grain buckets onto a wheelbarrow.

She could make this happen. She could win. Show Tim and her own mother how wrong they've been about her. Prove that she's not a mediocre rider, doomed to muck stalls for the *real* riders. Her education in computer science and her passable programming skills might only grant her an entry-level job if she were to apply to work for the big four—a handful of multimillion-dollar corporations that are the only employers left hiring. But just because that'd be good enough for Iris's mother doesn't mean that it's good enough for her. Because now, here in Timothy Walker's world, those same skills might just bring her the fame and fortune of winning the last Dressage World Cup and securing the riches it'll take to survive the looming catastrophe.

The barn's viewing room window is completely steamed up. Iris wipes a spot clean at the corner of the window, tapping her finger against the laptop's closed lid. It's late at night. She's just put in another sixteen-hour day.

In the arena, Tim talks to Tina, who sits atop the number one horse in the barn, Alfred. Iris has never had the pleasure of riding the stallion, even though she was promised the opportunity when she was hired to work for Mister Walker. But she and the horse still share a close bond; Iris is the one who feeds, grooms, and spends the most time with him. On those late nights when she feels herself crumbling under the pressure and the exhaustion, it's Alfred who listens to Iris's venting. Sitting in the corner of the stallion's stall, she watches him eat hay, telling him how badly she wants to give up but won't. And though the stallion hardly responds to her venting, he's always there, soft-eyed and calm, radiating unworldly comfort that Iris barely understands. Whatever the connection between them is, it's strong. Iris has even taught Alfred a few tricks, like "high five," where the stallion rears on his hind legs when Iris says the trigger word—"up!"

Tina stops in the center of the arena, where Tim stands. She throws her head back and laughs at something the trainer says to her, brown ponytail dancing around her narrow, muscular shoulders. When Tim grabs Tina by the boot with one hand, then places his other hand on her thigh, Tina gives him a knowing smile. She's only five years older than Iris, but in Iris's eyes, she acts closer to Tim's age. Forty-five? Fifty? Iris has always had a hard time estimating how old people are. The trainer's long mustache and bald head make him look older than he probably is. It's hard to tell when it comes to professional riders; their excellent fitness level makes most of them look younger than they are.

In the middle of the arena, Tim moves Tina's lower leg, placing it by the saddle's girth. He gestures at an invisible line that travels from the horse's mouth to Tina's elbow, and from there to Alfred's hind end. Tina's leg isn't positioned wrong; Iris, just like any advanced rider, would know. Yet, Timothy corrects her at the beginning of each lesson. Squeezing her thigh, Timothy moves Tina's boot back a few inches along the horse's side. When he slides his other hand higher on Tina's thigh, Iris's finger stops tapping the laptop. She stares at the scene intensely, holding her breath. As always, if Tina's bothered by her trainer's intimate touch, she doesn't let on.

As Tina nods at her trainer and the stallion finally moves on with his swinging gait, Iris lets out a long exhale. Her fingers return to their rapid drumming against the laptop's lid. The window steams over, and Iris moves her hand to wipe it off, then quickly changes her mind. She leans back in her seat and stares at the neat row of double-bridles hanging on wooden hooks on the wall.

Even if he finds the algorithm useful, she thinks, gripping the edge of the wooden bench she sits on. *Is it enough?*

Tina is Timothy's protégé. She moved away from America and over to Iceland with him and the horses. When Iris started working for him a year ago, she was more advanced in her dressage riding than Tina seemed to be. But even so, Iris has always seemed like an after-thought for Timothy, no matter how much work and effort she put in.

Staring off into space, Iris misses the sound of the viewing room door opening. It's not until Tim drops his riding gloves on the table with a loud *thud* that she snaps out of her thoughts.

"Night check done?"

Iris places both of her hands on the laptop, fingering its smooth lid. "All done," she replies. "I left Alfred's grain bucket outside his stall door. I'll stay and wait until he's ready for it."

A low grunt is all she gets for an answer. Tim shuffles a stack of papers in his hands, then pulls out a pen from his chest pocket to make a note. It looks like printed invoices, or maybe sign-up forms of some kind. Iris sits taller and wets her lips to ask but decides to keep her mouth shut instead. She takes short peeks at the man, her finger again tapping against the laptop. Out of the corner of her eye, she sees Alfred in silhouette walking past the viewing room window as Tina brings him back into the barn to put a fleece cooler on him.

"Would you cut that out?" Tim snaps without taking his gaze off the papers.

Iris's hand freezes. Slowly, she places her palm on the laptop. She wets her lips again.

The words stick in her throat. The mere thought of asking Tim a question terrifies her. It's not unlike him to explode over what seems like nothing—especially when Iris is around. She seems to be a trigger to him, hard for him to tolerate for longer than a few minutes at a time. This doesn't happen with Tina—or the rare occasional guests visiting the barn. Just Iris.

It's because you're worthless, she thinks. It's her familiar inner voice that comes around at moments like these, scolding her with its ruthless tone. *A fuck-up. No wonder you never get to ride Alfred. You can hardly hold a freaking counter canter for a full twenty-meter circle.*

She closes her eyes, knowing that her inner voice is just getting started. This is just the top of the roller-coaster, about to push forward into a free fall, listing all the fucks-ups she's made today and earlier this week. Earlier in her life.

You shouldn't even be allowed to exist in the same building as Timothy Walker. All you do is piss him off. Like that time when you put the wrong bridle on Whisper . . . what the hell were you thinking? Any nincompoop could see it was Shadow's noseband, the one with extra padding . . .

"I found an algorithm," Iris blurts out, just to interrupt her inner voice's joyride.

Tim closes his eyes, takes a breath, then lowers the hand that holds the papers. He opens his dull eyes and stares at Iris, his lips turned slightly downward. "A what now?"

Iris clears his throat. She nods at her laptop, then folds her fingers to stop her hands from shaking. She glances at Tim, then looks away at the bridle hooks. "I hacked into the Van Dijk Sport Horse database. I have access to their server and all the information stored there. A lot of it has to do with the World Cup." She forces herself to look back at Timothy to see his reaction.

Tim blinks twice. His brow furrows as he glances at Iris's laptop. "And?"

Iris takes a quick breath before continuing. "They use an algorithm to analyze each horse, rider, and training session at the barn. And not just riding, but feed, medication, rest, supplements, shoes . . . you name it."

For a moment, something that Iris has never seen before shadows Timothy's face. Not surprise, but . . . *approval.* He stares at Iris, rubbing his mustache with his thumb and index finger while thinking hard about

Iris's words. Heart racing, Iris forces herself to take a breath while she waits for him to say something.

Why would you do that? He's just going to tell you that all that information is useless. Useless—just like you. What kind of a moron . . .

"You said information about the World Cup . . ." he finally says, taking a slow step toward the table. "Which year? *This* year?"

Iris exhales and nods. "Yes. Preparations, the rider and horse participating, their compatibility, a full SWOT analysis, and detailed training schedule and nutritional plan."

Timothy takes the two steps separating him from the table. With stiff movements, he reaches for a chair, pulls it back with a loud *screech*, then sits down across from Iris. He leans one elbow against the table and cups his mouth and mustache with his palm, leaning against his hand.

A minute passes. Then another. Then thirty. At least that's what it feels like to Iris, as she waits for the man to react in some way. Almost wishing that Tim would just explode and yell at her until her face is covered with his spit, Iris zones out and enters her mental vessel. In her mind, she jumps into the laptop in front of her, dives into the network, changing her whole being into raw data with no feelings, no emotions. She travels across the ocean, line after line, one wireless router to another, all the way to the Netherlands. Just like the algorithm, she's now powerful. Strong. Something. *Someone.*

His hand lands on Iris's. She gives a start as she snaps back into the viewing room, blinking at the steamed-over glass and then Timothy's intense stare. She swallows hard, unable to turn her gaze from his. Something dark has taken over his eyes, but it's not the darkness that Iris notices in his expression. It's the faint smile twitching the corners of his lips. When he opens his mouth to speak, Iris can't help her panicky gasp.

"Well, well, well. Maybe you're not as dumb as you look, after all." His clammy palm pats Iris's hand twice, then pulls back as Timothy crosses his arms on his chest. He nods at Iris's computer. "Show me."

CHAPTER 3
THE RESORT
(5 YEARS EARLIER)

Her winter boots thump against the barn's wooden floor. Moonlight enters the building through the stall bars, throwing long shadows on the barn aisle. The horses lift their heads, some nickering uncertainly, some ignoring Iris completely. It's not feeding time. Tonight, she doesn't have night check. It's Thursday—her only day off.

Brisk, raw air slaps against her face as Iris walks out of the barn building. Across the yard, an enormous three-story house with a porch and balcony stands in the moonlight. The upper floor belongs to Tina; the two other floors are Timothy's alone. Tina has a separate entrance, but Iris sees her entering the house from Timothy's front door more often than not. In fact, she sees her downstairs more than upstairs in her own living quarters. Not that Iris means to stalk her or anything—it's just that the house has no curtains to block the clear view inside.

She walks over to the garage and heads for her bicycle with its brand new studded winter tires. As she swings her leg over and is about to ride off, her gaze locks with the main house's living room window. Iris gasps for air and freezes to watch.

Tina sits on the couch, her chin tucked in and arms resting at her sides, palms pointing up. Timothy stands behind her, rubbing her shoulders, circling his thumbs on her collar bones. Tina sits still, not smiling, not talking. When Tim lowers his hands toward Tina's V-neck, Iris gasps again, this time inhaling wrong. She doubles over, coughing loudly. When she gathers herself enough to look up again, the couple inside the house is staring out the window, listening.

Iris kicks the bike forward and starts pedaling down the driveway as hard as her exhausted legs will let her. Her intermittent breath in her ears, she makes her way down to the lava fields, forcing herself to focus on the winding road instead of her raging, restless thoughts. The farther from the farm she gets, the more even her breathing becomes. When she sees the blue lagoon glimmering in the moonlight, she's utterly lost in her mental vessel, somewhere far away from this place, from this life, from herself. She focuses on the turquoise water, trying to block out the hotel rising in the distance. For a minute or two, she can just stay in this moment. For a tiny while longer, she isn't a nobody with calluses and bunions, working for something that she might never achieve. Right now, in this time and place, there is no Tina. No Timothy Walker.

For a fleeting moment longer, she's not about to meet with her mother for a late-night dinner.

"Fix your napkin, Iris." The woman with green highlights in her hair and too much makeup on—Iris's mother—dabs her pink lips with her own napkin while giving Iris a disapproving look. "How am I ever going to bring you to the yacht club to meet a decent bachelor when you can't even dine without embarrassing me?"

Iris chews on her tofu steak, dodging her mother's gaze. This is hardly the first or the last time she's pressured Iris to take a new direction in her life. A ten-year-plan. That's what she needs, according to the woman sitting in front of her.

"Iris?"

"Yeah, I heard you."

"And?"

"And . . . " she says and looks down to work with her fork and knife, cutting another piece of steak. She puts the knife down against the plate with a clank, then digs her fork into the bigger part of the steak and brings it to her lips. Before she takes a bite, she says, "And the yacht club isn't really my scene."

"Well that's only because you've never given it a fair shot. No one will approach a Negative Nelly with no table manners . . . Jesus Mary and Joseph, would you put that down?" her mother nods at the chunk of steak, "Immediately."

Iris hesitates for a moment, keeping her gaze on her mother, but then takes a mouthful and sets the steak down on the plate. Struggling to chew on the large piece of soy meat, she brings her hand to her mouth and wipes off the drippings. "It's just not for me," she replies once her mouth is less full, catching herself just in time before she sets her elbow on the table.

"Well, as disappointing as that is to hear," her mother says, reaching for a piece of bread. "I can't say that I'm surprised."

Iris clears her throat. After a soothing breath, she asks, "And why is that?"

"Because you turn your nose up at any intelligent suggestion ever brought in front of you. You always have. Even as a child, you would put up your fists at any given opportunity, instead of hearing and learning from those who know better than you."

Iris takes another breath, then counts to six. "I've made progress with my riding," she says, fully aware of how clumsily she tries to offer her mother something to be proud of.

"Yeah?" her lipstick-covered mouth mutters half-heartedly. She checks the time on her wristwatch.

"Yeah, if there were still national competitions going, I would score best in any class."

"Pff…"

Iris opens her mouth, but then sucks in her lips. The offer hasn't gone through. It won't go through. Anything that is actually, genuinely her, will never be good enough for her mother. That fist-fighting young Iris now screams inside her, waving her hands, jumping, stomping. "I'm not worthless," she cries with tears and snot streaking her little face. "You just can't see me! Look at me. The *real* me. Open your eyes … See me."

To give her nervous hands something to do, she gulps down the glass of sparkling water in front of her, then sets the empty glass on the table, staring at it instead of meeting her mother's irritated gaze. Iris already knows how the rest of the conversation will go. She knows how it'll end too. Both of them do. After years of pushing each other's buttons, trying to change each other's point of view, all they've managed is to create a battlefield with no winners or losers. To save them both some time, Iris decides to jump forward and push her mother's biggest button and skip the rest.

"So I should just find a man to support me? Is that it?"

"Oh, stop that. You make it sound like I'm sending you to a butcher."

"Marriage?" Iris continues, ignoring her mother's words. "Isn't that a thing of the past now? Everybody and their mother have gotten divorced a long time ago. If people are brave enough to meet a stranger, they'd rather do that online and never meet face to face."

"Not everyone," her mother says sulkily. "Not the inner circle."

"Oh, so the yacht club is like, what? A pimp for traditional values and expired concepts?"

"Call it whatever you want, Iris." Her mother fixes her hair, puffing the hairspray-covered chignon. "Intelligent people know that sticking with the old ways is the way to survive in today's ludicrous world."

"What if I don't need a man to take care of me?" Iris is proud that her voice isn't shivering, even though her skin feels inflamed by the rage she's trying to press down. "Just because you used Olav's connections to get ahead in life, doesn't mean I have to do the same."

Her mother stops chewing, her face momentarily frozen in a strange expression. Soon, she attacks her shrimp salad with her fork, as though it's the salad being rude to her, not Iris. "Would it kill you to call him *dad*?" she says slowly, her voice filled with hurt and bottled-up feelings. "Just because he's no longer with us doesn't change things."

Without looking up, Iris works on her steak. *It changes everything*, she thinks. *For the better*. Hands shaking, she swallows painfully, trying to ignore the nauseating feeling in her guts.

"My coworker has a bachelor son," her mother says, completely oblivious to Iris's nausea. "He works for the big four and will relocate to Switzerland in a few months. If you'd put on a dress and come—"

"I don't own a dress."

"Then we'll buy you one. With the right attitude, you might even convince him to overlook some of your . . . *shortcomings* and give it a shot."

Iris looks up from her plate, grinding her teeth. She doesn't need to ask what shortcomings it is her mother is talking about. Because if she did, the woman would only half-heartedly wave in the general direction of Iris's whole damn life. "I appreciate the offer," she says between her teeth. "But I think I'll pass."

"You always do this."

"Do what?"

"Embarrass me. Go against my word."

"No I don't."

"Yes, you do. I told you not to go work for that Yankee with the ridiculous mustache, and what do you do? You go work for the Yankee with the ridiculous mustache. I tell you to wear more makeup now that I've finally fixed your hair and made you somewhat decent-looking. And what do you do? You show up here with a clean, pale face. I tell you to apply for a *real* job with one of the big four. And what do you know—you trash all the applications I was kind enough to send your way."

Iris nods a few times, pointing at her full mouth, then lifting a finger to gesture she needs a moment to finish her bite. Her frustration level is rising dangerously high. She still has a big ask to present, and even without giving her mother any attitude whatsoever, it'll be fool's luck if her mother agrees to give her more money.

A waiter with a sly smile walks over to fill Iris's water glass. He glances at Iris's trembling hands but doesn't comment on them. After the finest bow, he backs away, leaving Iris to gulp down the bubbly water.

"Well," her mother huffs while pushing a piece of shrimp back and forth on her plate, "what do you have to say for yourself?"

Iris wipes her mouth on the back of her palm, reaches for the napkin on her lap, and theatrically lets it drop on her plate. She crosses her arms on the table and leans in closer to her mom, giving her a quick smile. Every time she looks at the woman, defiance lifts its ugly head, pushing her further and further away from leaving this dinner with any money in her pockets.

"Well," she says in a low voice. Then she clears her throat and leans back in her chair, throwing her arm over the backrest. "I mean . . . " She spreads her hands once, then lets them relax again. "If you want me to fuck a sailor," she says, her voice loud and clear, "I'll fuck a sailor. No problem."

A pink flush appears at the top of her mother's cheeks, radiating through the thick layer of makeup. Her eyes widening in shock, she stares at Iris. Something other than embarrassment shadows her face.

Hurt.

Iris winces at the look on her face. Though her mother and Iris hardly see eye to eye—and not just on who she dates or doesn't date, but on most things in life—it also turns her stomach to see her mother hurting. Why can't she just play along? Do as she's told? Maybe then, just once, her mother would look at her with something other than resentfulness and embarrassment in her eyes.

Iris sucks her lower lip in, glancing around the restaurant. The people around them are seemingly focused on their tablets and phones, but Iris catches a few of them side-eyeing their table. Her little scene hasn't gone unnoticed by anyone.

She takes a deep breath and picks up her silverware, releasing the steak from the fork's tines. "How's the cruise ship treating you?" she asks in a softer voice. "Business good as usual?"

Again playing with the shrimp on her plate, Iris's mother peers up at her. She's clearly eager to speak about her hair and makeup business that is—in her words—*booming* among the VRPs, the very rich persons. She's hoping to retire in one of the billionaire villages at one of the classified locations. Her specialty is real-life makeup that resembles your Avatar on the new VR simulations the VRP's are spending more and more of their time in. Iris doesn't understand much of it, but she's relieved that, unlike most older people, her mother hadn't needed to quit working when the unemployment rates skyrocketed, leaving most people completely dependent on their failing government and their negligible aid programs.

"Business is good," her mother replies, trying to keep her voice cool. She's not one to let Iris go easy once she's crossed a boundary as extreme as shouting obscenities. Reputation comes first in her mother's world, and that includes her no-good, manure-smelling, pale-faced daughter. "I'm only fifteen credits from the retirement fund, actually."

"Oh yeah?"

Her mother can't help a quick grin. "Yes. Nothing's confirmed, but the cruise ship CEO let me understand that I'll be retiring somewhere warm. With cocktails and a swimming pool."

"Sounds very posh, Mamma."

Her burgundy painted eyelids blink rapidly as she looks at Iris, resentment in her gaze. "Mother," she corrects Iris. "We speak English in this family. And English only." She pauses to scoff. "You should know better."

The anger that has simmered somewhere beneath her skin now starts to boil. "You're right." Iris drops her fork and knife on the plate, then pushes the plate forward on the table. "Let me add that to my list of shortcomings and fuckups. Is this priority number one? Hm? Poor language skills over occupation and lack of retirement plan?"

"Don't be so . . . so *vulgar*."

Iris fails to stifle the giggle provoked by her mother's words. "*That's* vulgar to you?" She pauses, this time sucking her lower lip in to stop the mocking laughter bubbling at the back of her throat. She takes a quick sip of water, leans back, and crosses her arms on her chest, casting a longing glance at the door that leads to the hotel lobby and out of the building. "And here I thought you limited *vulgar* to rinsing and cleaning Alfred's sheath and balls. Is that an okay conversation topic now? Horse junk? I mean, as long as the conversation happens in the grammatically correct English language?"

Way out of line, she thinks, closing her eyes, regret washing over her. *Way,* way *out.*

Her mother blinks at Iris rapidly, her mouth popping open. Iris notices a smudge of pink lipstick on her mother's slightly protruding upper teeth.

Iris closes her eyes and breathes in. "I'm sorry, Mother," she says without opening her eyes. "I didn't mean to upset you." She breathes out and opens her eyes, staring at her mother, who avoids her gaze. "Things are . . . *tough* around the barn. I'm under a lot of stress. And you know that's hard for me to admit."

Her mother wipes an invisible tear from the corner of her eye. After a faint sniff, she turns to look at Iris, her usual stern expression once again covering her face. "Of course it's stressful. It's abuse, not a job. What did you expect? I told you not to work for that man. He's bad news."

Her heart missing a beat, Iris opens her mouth to disagree, then clamps it shut in confusion. Why does she have such a strong urge to defend Timothy? Her mother knows nothing of the way the man talks to

Iris. She doesn't know about the threats of violence if she doesn't get her tempi changes right. She's never seen the inappropriate way he looks at Tina, or the way his thumbs travel down her collarbones . . .

"Iris?"

She shakes her head to get rid of the images. "Yeah, yeah. He's an egoistic asshole with a god complex. I know. But he's also the best of the best. If I get to ride for him in the World Cup, I'll make enough money to stay in Iceland, and I won't have to emigrate—"

"I'm sorry," her mother interrupts Iris's sentence. "What do you mean *if* you get to ride in the World Cup?" She gasps for air dramatically. "You're saying it's not a done deal?!"

Shit. Balls. Fuck. Fuck. Fuck.

"No, of course it's a done deal. I just meant . . . "

"Oh my heavens. He's going to give that Yankee chick your spot, isn't he?"

"No . . . "

After another loud gasp for air, Iris's mother cups her mouth and looks away. "A whole year wasted." She lets out a sob which could be fake or real. "My only daughter, shoveling manure. Living in a filthy, rat-infested barn when she could use the education I so generously paid for to become a productive member of society. But no. Instead, she insists on working for a foreign sadist who marches into

Reykjavik like he owns the place. And for what? Just to play with ponies while undermining and belittling the good people who have lived here long before he was ever born."

"Mother . . ."

"And all this time I thought," she pauses for another sob, "at least it'll all come to an end once this World Cup takes place and she wins herself a decent amount of money. Maybe then I won't have to worry about her inhaling black mold all day long, working nine hours a day and getting paid for six."

Man, oh man, she thinks. *I wish her math was right.*

"About that . . ." Iris starts, then pauses to take a slow sip of water. It'll be her mother's turn to cause a scene. She knows that already. Maybe she shouldn't ask . . . but the rent is due tomorrow. And if Timothy doesn't get his money on time, Iris's life will become intolerable. More so than it already is. "I could use . . . a loan." She bites her lower lip before continuing with a weak voice. "A small one, and just for a month . . . or two."

Her chest heaving, her mother takes a deep breath. With a robust but shaky voice, she asks, "But your stipend? What could you possibly need money for when you work nine hours a day and never leave the barn? You don't buy new clothes. You don't go out with friends. Take vacations. You are skin and bones, so you barely eat. Where does all your money go?"

Iris holds her breath. She's never told her mother that she pays to ride Timothy's horses, not the other way around. One forty-five-minute lesson with one of the world's best trainers isn't cheap either. And it's not just that. It's been two months since Timothy decided to raise the rent on her room, making it so that Iris's stipend didn't cover the cost of training and living at the barn.

"I'll pay it back," she says, dodging her mother's questioning gaze. Finally, she waves her mother off with a hostile hand movement. "Never mind. It's not a big deal. I can always just come here late Friday and Saturday night and sell my ass. Not that there are many tourists left to whore out to . . ."

Iris's mother bounces up from her seat, her chair clattering backward. Her pink lips open, then close, making her look like a fish left to die by the Reykjavik harbor fishing docks. Iris's whole body goes stiff as she waits for what's about to come. People stare at them, no longer bothering to be discreet.

Now you've gone and done it, ass-face. If she slaps you around, it's well-deserved. What kind of a person acts like this, especially when you know very well that she suffers from high blood pressure . . .

Iris swallows as her mother takes a step closer to the table. But instead of attacking Iris, she reaches for her purse, takes out a strange-looking set of what must be

VR glasses. As she puts them on, the sly waiter hurries to their table, mirroring Iris's mother by shoving an identical pair of glasses on his face.

"Paying in Chip-Currency?"

"Yes, please," her mother answers the waiter, her voice more high-pitched and shaky than usual.

After a moment of tapping the glasses, the two of them nod at each other approvingly, ending their odd exchange. The waiter clears his throat and gives Iris a polite smile. "All done with this, madam?" he asks, gesturing at Iris's plate and the pierced steak. All she can do is nod.

Her mother takes off the strange glasses, shoves them into her purse, and turns to look at Iris. Her eyes ice-cold, she says, "You want money? Get a job. A *real* job. If you apply for a position with one of the big four, we can talk about a loan. Until then, I don't care what you do. I don't want to see you, hear you, remember you. Not until you come to your senses and start acting like an actual human being, and not some filthy barn rat that is shaming her whole family."

Iris wants to ask "what family" as she and her mother are the only ones left in Iceland. Everyone else, Aunt Lilja and her husband Gunnar, as well as Iris's forever-bachelor uncle Björn, have moved to random places somewhere in central Europe to live off the united government—the same government that is quickly running out of housing and losing the ability to relocate so many people who have lost their jobs, houses, and any hope to excel in life. The relocation hubs they've been sent to sound beyond shady to Iris—as does the fact that no one is allowed to contact people outside the hubs—but she seems to be the only one filled with questions and skepticism.

Iris exhales and stands up from her seat. "Mamma . . ." Against her usual ways, she walks to her mother and reaches for her hands. The long, plastic nails dig slightly into Iris's palms as she cups her mother's hands in hers. "Mamma, please. It's only temporary. The Cup is only two months away. Once I win . . ."

"Once you win," her mother says, then blows a raspberry. She pulls her hands away from Iris's touch as if she's carrying a deadly virus. "Even if you did go to your little competition and somehow managed to win. So what? You'll still be what you are today. A person with no real skills. No retirement plan. No place in the new society. You think people will look at you differently after you've won some silly sporting event in the Netherlands?" Her mother blows another raspberry. "Please. Anyone who's anything knows that sports are a thing of the past. Nothing important. A waste of resources and people's time. If it ever was anything else in the first place."

"Mamma," Iris whispers again and closes her eyes, willing herself to keep it together. The back of her eyes burn, partly out of anger, partly out of the hurt of her own mother disowning her in the middle of a public restaurant. "Please."

Her pink lips open, then shut again. Her chin lifted, Iris's mother narrows her eyes and whispers, "Get yourself together, woman. Find yourself a man to support you, or go find a real job. Until you do one or the other, you are as good as dead to me."

The bathroom light changes from neon blue to neon green. Iris blows her nose and hugs her arms around her knees on the toilet seat. Leaning her forehead against her knees, she tries another deep breath. How long has she been sitting here? Since her mother paid for dinner—but not her rent—and then turned around and walked out of Iris's life?

Thirty minutes?

An hour?

Four?

The resort and its hotel are open twenty-four-seven. The tourists who come here are either taking the cruise Iris's mother works for or they are regular VRPs traveling around the last few safe destinations in Europe. Yet no one has entered the women's room for the whole time Iris has been here. She should head back to the barn. It may be her only day off, but come five a.m., she needs to be back at it.

She blows her nose again, gets up, and tosses the paper in the trash. The booth door swooshes open smoothly. Iris walks to the glowing wall behind a giant mirror with invisible speakers playing soothing forest sounds. After rinsing her face, she leaves the bathroom and heads back to the restaurant.

The tables are all empty. She walks to peek in at the bar, only to find that space empty as well. If there is anyone still drinking their worries away, they must be in the bar up on the roof level. Iris glances at the digital clock above the bar.

01:58

"Fuck me sideways . . ." she mutters and quickens her step. She needs to be feeding morning hay and grain in just three short hours. She hurries to the hotel lobby, but a strange feeling stops her just as she's about to leave the hotel and fetch her bike from the court-yard. Her hand on the front door's open button, Iris freezes in place to listen. But she hears nothing. No music. No talking. Nothing. Yet, she can't help feeling she's being watched.

She turns around to stare at a huge house plant sitting in the corner of the lobby. Something moves in the shadows. Then, from behind the plant, someone steps out into the dim light of the corridor. Her white lab shoes stop where the corridor and the lobby's entryway meet. Holding a martini glass in one hand, a blonde woman with clear, striking eyes crosses her free arm over her stomach. She tilts her head, investigating Iris's face.

"You know how to pick a lock?"

Iris lowers her hand and steps back from the door. Frowning, she does her best to process the strange conversation opener. Her eyes sting from crying in the bathroom, and the memory of her mother's disappointed face makes her sick to her stomach. She should go home. Just . . . leave. But something about this lady and her strange confidence inspires Iris to take another step away from the front door. "What kind of lock?"

"Oh, you know." The woman, whose white doctor's coat is puzzling given the hour and her present occupation, lifts her full glass at Iris, then walks over, passes Iris, and continues to a door at the side of the lobby. She nods at the door, then turns to talk to Iris. "The old-fashioned kind. But a sturdy one. Made in Finland, you see."

Iris stares at the door and the woman standing next to it, but she doesn't move closer. "What does Finland have to do with it? Did they invent the world's first lock or something?"

Her dry, brief laughter fills the lobby. Staring at the lock, the woman mumbles, "Sisu, sauna, Sibelius, and locks . . . " She seems to have momentarily forgotten that Iris is in the room. "Doesn't really rhyme as nicely."

Iris frowns and takes a step closer. "What's that?"

"Nothing . . . dear." The endearment sounds off, as if she's trying on a pair of new shoes that don't quite fit, but she's decided to stick with them anyway. She turns to face Iris. "The morons who moved in the equipment forgot to remove the hardware lock when they placed the CS-key on the door." She knocks on the door twice. "The damn thing double-locks, and I can only open the digital one."

"What's down there?" Iris asks, immediately biting her tongue. She should just leave. Leave this odd stranger alone and bike back home. But her feet won't move. She can't stop admiring the woman's calm, confident movements, the way she stands tall and strong as if she's some kind of an indestructible force. And that force pulls Iris in like a magnet. It's easy to be near her. Tempting. Almost as if Iris could absorb some of that radiating power and keep it for herself.

"My life's work," the woman says. She lifts the martini glass in her hand, as if it has suddenly started to bug her. "That's what's down there." Drops of martini spill on the lobby floor as the woman's light gait takes her away from the door. "Or, I guess not just my life's work," she continues, this time her voice taking on a darker tone. "But my mother's as well."

"Your mother invented the lock?" Iris tries a joke, then scolds herself for such a poor attempt at humor. "Is she from Finland?" she asks quickly, as if to scratch her first question.

"She invented something, alright. The great Marjaana Salonen . . . " With slow, light steps, she walks back to the house plant in the corner and stops to stare at it. She leans over and pours the drink into the soil, then drops the empty martini glass into the dirt in the plant pot. "And her healing powers."

Iris stares at the plant, then at the woman who now leans her back against the lobby wall, scoffing silently at her own thoughts.

This woman is clearly insane, her inner voice appears out of nowhere, as it so often does. *Just leave her crazy ass here and go home.*

Iris takes a step back toward the front door, but the woman's voice stops her.

"What difference does it make," she says slowly, still staring at the ceiling and leaning against the wall, "what *kind* of a lock?"

"What?"

Her hands folded behind her back, the woman peers at Iris, giving her a small smile. She starts walking around the lobby slowly, ghostly, like the draft that travels through Iris's room at night. "I asked you if you can pick a lock . . . "

"Right," Iris says, hesitation in her voice. "And?"

"And you asked what kind of a lock. Why?"

"If it was a biometric lock or a digital one, I could open it." Iris frowns at her own words. Why is she still here, explaining herself to this weird stranger?

"Huh," the woman says. She stops her relaxed strolling around the lobby, her back turned to Iris. When she turns around and tilts her head, something new twinkles in her blue eyes: curiosity. "You can hack into things?"

Iris shifts her weight from one foot to another. When her words get stuck in her throat, all she can do is nod.

"Want a job?" the woman asks then, her facial expression far from motherly or authoritative, but . . . *approving*.

Iris scoffs and glances at the front door. "Doing what? Breaking into hotels?"

"Is it really breaking in," she asks and walks back to the double-locked door. "If what's inside is already yours?"

She points at a small sign made of cardboard next to the door. A piece of duct tape holds it up. The hand-written text is hard to read. Iris squints her eyes but struggles to read the text because of the distance and dim lighting. She can't help it—she walks over to read what it says.

"Doctor Laura Solomon," Iris reads aloud. "ICE Laboratory."

She takes an immediate step back from Doctor Solomon. Eyes wide, Iris stares at the woman. "I've, um . . ."

"Let me guess," Laura says with a dry smile. "You've *heard* things. About me. Rumors."

"I have . . . " Iris says slowly. "But that's not what I was about to say."

"What, then?"

Thoughts twirl in Iris's mind. This woman is a world-renowned scientist. A genius. But she's also known to be an egotistical maniac with a vision of some kind of a cult where people would all live, act, and think in one way and one way only.

Doctor Solomon's way.

"I've got to go." Iris turns around and storms out the hotel's front door. She runs down the court-yard and off to the driveway—only to remember that she's forgotten her bike. She turns around and runs back, her frantic thoughts stopping her from seeing clearly. Finally, she stops, realizing she's somehow taken a wrong turn while running back for her bike. A sight she's never seen at the resort before opens in front of her. A familiar sight. *Very* familiar.

Hay bales.

Grain bags.

Horses.

How did she not see them when biking in tonight? How far away in her own world had she been?

The silhouette of a woman with a bicycle appears from around the corner. With steady, easy steps, Doctor Solomon walks Iris's bike over to her. As she gestures for Iris to grab the bars, she digs out something from her white coat pocket.

A business card.

"It doesn't have to be a breaking into stuff kind of a job," Laura says, pronouncing the end of her sentence carefully. "There's a lot to do around here, now that I've taken over. Tasks that need a person with a special set of skills."

Startled by the sight of horses in the moonlight, Iris accepts the business card. She stares at it for a while, then looks up at Laura. "Like barn work?"

"Among other things." She shrugs a shoulder. "Sure."

What the fuck is wrong with you? Iris's inner voice interrupts her, staring into those ice-cold, compelling eyes. *No. You are not considering her offer. World Cup. Retirement. Fortune and fame. That's the plan. That's what you need to focus on. Not working for some maniac who hides martini glasses in houseplants.*

"I got to go," Iris breathes out. As she grabs the bike with both hands, Laura's business card lands on the courtyard's cobblestone ground. Hastily, she rides off, never looking back to see if Laura Solomon stares after her with resentment in her eyes, like her mother would.

A pitchfork in her hand, Iris fast-walks through the arena, wincing at the sound of Timothy's scream. Foaming and puffing, Alfred canters toward Iris. She stops, waits for the horse to go around her, and then continues to the steaming manure pile she's about to pick up. Tina's face is red, Iris notices. Redder than usual. And that's not the only anomaly, she thinks as she picks the poop up and shakes the pitchfork slightly to rid it of any sand and rubber footing stuck on the droppings.

Timothy never screams at *Tina*.

With quick steps, Iris heads to the bucket at the corner of the arena. After dumping the poop in the bucket, she hangs the pitchfork back on the wall's metal hook. Just as she's about to walk back into the aisle to finish the night check, she hears Tim yell her name.

Shit.

She freezes in the doorway and takes a few seconds before turning around.

"What the hell are you standing there for?" his booming voice fills the arena. Alfred has stopped moving around. "Get your ass over here."

Iris turns. Hesitantly, she starts toward the horse and the two people in the middle of the arena. Tina is out of breath, and her face lacks its usual smirking confidence. When the stallion moves under her seat without asking, she hisses at him and kicks him with her left foot. Iris winces in sync with the horse.

Timothy turns to stare at Tina. "And why, in the name of all untalented, crappy, fuckturd riders in this world, are you kicking *him*? You think it's the horse's fault you can't get this right?" He moves closer to the horse and takes the reins. "Get off."

"Tim, I can do it," Tina says. "Just let me try one more time."

His head jerks back at Tina's words. For a moment, all he does is stare at the rider up in the saddle. Iris stops at a safe distance, unsure of what to do. So she stands, twisting her hands uncomfortably. Timothy takes a breath, pats the horse's neck, and steps back. In a seemingly relaxed manner, he nods at Tina repeatedly as if to tell her that he's considering her request.

"Let me get this straight," he says in a calmer voice. "You have been running around in a twenty-meter circle for forty minutes straight." He pauses as his voice starts to rise. "Trying and trying and *trying* to get your two tempis right. While I'm standing here . . ." he grabs onto both ends of the dressage whip in his hands, "like some worthless *asshole*, doing my best to figure out why it's so goddamn hard to perform this simple as *fuck* task without fucking it up every single *fucking* time!"

Timothy's moved closer to Tina. If she wasn't sitting so high up on the horse, Tim's spit would land on her red, terrified face.

"And now you . . ." he stops talking to shake his head and scoff, "you want to *try* . . . again?" He squeezes the whip in his hands, bending it like a twig until it snaps in two. "Get! The fuck! *Off*!"

Tina kicks off the stirrups, swings her right leg over, and lands smoothly on two feet next to Alfred. The horse has evened out his breath, and not even the sound of the whip breaking has startled him. He must be used to Timothy acting this way, his nerves cool as can be.

Unlike Tina.

Unlike Iris.

Timothy turns his back on Tina and the horse. He starts walking back toward his coach's chair by the arena entryway. As he passes Iris, he waves the whip pieces at her half-heartedly. "Twenty-meter circle," he murmurs. "Two tempis. Left lead."

Iris wants to point out that she's not dressed to ride; She's wearing jeans, a sweater-jacket, and a pair of sneakers. She doesn't even have a helmet. Legs now full-on shaking, she takes the few steps that separate her from the stallion. Tina takes off her helmet, her thick brown hair soaked in sweat. She pushes the helmet into Iris's hands, then the reins.

"Congratulations," she hisses at Iris in a voice low enough that Timothy can't hear. "I hope you have what it takes to follow through."

Iris puts the wet helmet on and throws the reins over Alfred's neck. Though she's nervous and shaky, Tina's snarky comment gives her a second wind. "It's like he said," Iris says back to Tina without looking at her. She places her left foot in the stirrup and swings herself up on the saddle with ease. "It *should* be easy. How are you going to do your ones at the Cup, if you can't do your twos at home?"

The red in Tina's face deepens. She takes a step closer and pretends to scratch Alfred's neck. When she lifts her gaze to look at Iris, tears of rage glimmer in her eyes. "I'm not talking about the fucking tempis."

She side-eyes the trainer standing by his chair, arms crossed and tapping his boot in the sand. "I'm talking about him."

The barn fills with the sound of horses munching on their late-night hay. Tina has finished night check for Iris and left the barn, probably to lick her wounds and collect her shattered ego up in her heated apartment. Iris closes Alfred's stall door and double checks the latch. She's done perfectly. Better than she's ever ridden before. Maybe it was the stallion, maybe her once-in-a-lifetime chance to prove her worth to Timothy. Whatever it was that drove her tonight, it worked. Even Tim had nodded approvingly at her, once she let the stallion walk with a long rein around the arena.

"Come here for a second."

His voice gives Iris a start. She thought Tim had left the barn already, followed Tina inside to have his nightly glass of whisky. But as Iris turns toward the sound, she sees Tim leaning against the viewing room doorframe, his arms crossed on his chest. No smile. But something about his face has changed. The way he looks at Iris now is new.

Iris walks over and follows Tim into the viewing room. On the table, her laptop is turned on, the lid open, her notes open on the screen.

"Walk me through this again," he says, sits down at the table, then pats a spot next to him on the wooden bench. "I don't care about Germany or France or any of the other barns. Just show me Van Dijk's stuff again."

"The algorithm?" Iris asks. She tries not to hold her breath as she walks over and sits next to the man. She reaches for the laptop so she can move it closer to her, but Tim grabs onto it and places it right in front of him, forcing Iris to lean close to him to reach for the keyboard.

"Just . . . " he says and scratches his balding head. "Just the training program. And the test scores." He chuckles a bit, then leans his head against his palm, looking at Iris with eyes that could almost be described as . . . friendly.

She taps on the keyboard, very aware of how close to her trainer she has to lean. Her need—and right— to move her own laptop in whatever direction she wants shouldn't make her self-conscious—but it does. Whenever she's close to Timothy, all her confidence and smarts seem to vanish.

"This is the latest score for Jetta . . . " Iris mumbles, keeping her gaze on the screen. She feels Timothy moving even closer, his shoulder brushing hers.

"Who's the rider again?"

"Luuk Visser," Iris says, her eyes scanning the information on the screen. "His average on the test is forty . . ."

Iris stops talking and freezes when Tim's hand brushes a loose lock of blue hair off Iris's face and tucks it behind her ear. She swallows, then holds her breath.

What the fuck is this?

"Go on," Timothy says, his voice raspy. "What was the latest score?"

Iris swallows again, trying to ignore his hand that now rests on her shoulder. She forces a shallow breath and types in a command. Then she copy-pastes the information to her notes and continues reading, "The latest training session was today. Jetta and Visser, forty-five minutes, three sets of test programs . . ."

"The scores?" Timothy asks and drops his hand to Iris's thigh.

Frozen, struggling to keep her breathing even, Iris closes her eyes for two seconds. She forces herself to ignore the weight of Timothy's hand against her leg. All she wants to do is let her mind enter her mental vessel, so she can travel far away from here. But then she'd lose her chance.

"Thirty-eight," she hears her surprisingly steady voice saying, "Second round, thirty-nine. Third round . . ."

His hand moves away. Iris can't help it: she lets out a sigh of relief.

"What did you think of Alfred?" Timothy asks, investigating Iris's face as she stares at the screen.

She leans back and pulls her hands from the keyboard to gain some distance from the man. "I, um . . . I adore him."

"Impressive, isn't he?"

Iris nods.

"There's nothing like a powerful stallion that wants to please you. People think they are aggressive, straight up dangerous, even. But the truth is that they're sensitive. Just so fucking . . . " He pauses to find the right word, his hand circling in the air and eyes shining with admiration, "Delicate." He nods at his choice of word, then turns toward Iris a bit more. "Have you ever sat on one before?"

Iris forces a breath, then glances at the computer screen again, just to take a break from Timothy's intense stare. "A stallion?" she asks. When Tim doesn't answer but just keeps watching her with gleaming eyes, she hurries to say, "Not that I can remember. I used to come in for clinics and shows and warm up people's horses for money. One of them could have been a stallion, but . . . "

He reaches for her hair again. When Iris shies away from his touch, Tim's hand freezes midair.

Something dark flashes in his eyes when he pulls his hand away. "You know . . ." he says with a low, raspy voice, "Considering what happened in that arena today . . . seeing your dedication and willingness to go the extra mile . . . I might have to reconsider who's going to ride Alfred in the Cup."

The feeling starts deep in her stomach, traveling slowly up toward her chest. Butterflies. Ants. Something. Millions of tiny vibrations spread all around her body. Iris feels as if she's suddenly five inches taller.

"Oh, you'd like that," Timothy says, watching Iris's reaction. "Wouldn't you?"

Iris parts her lips to speak, but the excitement is too much for her to form words. All her hard work. All her sacrifice. The sixteen-hour shifts, mucking, grooming, cleaning, fixing, carrying water, cleaning drains . . . Not to prove her mother wrong. Not even to show Timothy what she's made of.

But to ride in the last ever Dressage World Cup. To win it.

"Well," he says and stretches his tall, slim frame. He gets up and takes a step toward the door. "Let me sleep on it. A night or two. I mean, we both know that Tina turned out to be a major disappointment."

While he takes a break to theatrically shake his head, Iris tries to remember what Tina did wrong during the two tempis. She had a few minutes to watch her ride while picking the manure up off the track. But nothing Tina had done seemed to have gone wrong. Tina might not be as good as Iris, but she's still damn good. But tonight, nothing she did seemed to please Timothy. The more she tried, repeating the same movements over and over, the more Timothy yelled, making Tina more and more flustered. *That's* when she started to make mistakes.

Deep in thought, Iris starts when Tim's hand cups her chin. His fingers clamp onto her face with a bit too much force, causing Iris to freeze in discomfort.

"But at the end of the day," he says slowly, staring into Iris with borderline hostile eyes, "I want to see you prove your commitment. Not just to Alfred, but to me. I want to make sure this wasn't some kind of a one-night thing—a magical mishap that caught me off guard." He leans even closer, his breath hot on Iris's face. "At the end of the day . . . it all comes down to how you and I get along . . . on a personal level."

CHAPTER 4
KNOCK ON THE DOOR
(5 YEARS EARLIER)

Tears burning her eyes, Iris stares at the message on her phone. It's from her mother, the only person who ever messages her anymore. She reads the words one more time, trying to convince herself that the tears are from relief, not from pain or sorrow.

I'VE BEEN SELECTED FOR THE RETIREMENT PROGRAM. I'M LEAVING TOMORROW MORNING, TEN O'CLOCK, SHARP. I WILL SEND YOU MONEY FOR RENT, BUT THIS WILL BE THE LAST TIME.

She wipes her eyes on the backs of her palms. She's not crying because her mother won't lend her money again. Anyone who moves away from Iceland is banned from staying in contact with those who have stayed put. Iris is not sure why, but she knows this will also be the case with her mother, now that she's retiring to one of the billionaire villages.

The pillow feels rough when Iris presses her face into it. She screams, trying to let out the pain that bubbles against her chest. With clenched fists, she squeezes the pillow, then tosses it aside and grabs her phone off the mattress. As hard as she can, Iris throws the phone against the wall. The screen cracks, but that's not good enough. With a few quick strides, she makes her way to her bedroom door, kicks on her steel-toed boots, and heads back to the phone. She steps on it hard. Twisting her feet from side to side, she pushes the phone against the hard floor, then stomps on it once, twice, three times for good measure.

The hollow feeling grows in her chest. Her knees give in, sending Iris down to the floor to sob uncontrollably. She's all alone. Everyone she ever cared about—gone. Anyone who could help her if things were to go terribly wrong has left Iceland and fled to places where Iris can't reach them anymore.

"Gutless traitors . . ." she says aloud and swallows hard. The sobs subside, and a new feeling takes over, first her body, then her mind. The feeling tickles the bottom of her stomach, then spreads like wildfire around her body, making it hard to breathe. Narrowing her eyes, Iris stares at what's left of her phone. She lets the rage engulf her, feeling its power thickening her skin as it burns her from inside out.

No more crying, her inner voice says, making Iris nod in agreement. *No more wallowing over cowards who give up on their home country. Their lives. Their dreams. Their freedom. Let them. Let her mother choke on her margarita by the pool. Let the rest of her family rot in some gray, concrete-box building in a place where it always rains. Or scorch their skins in a ripped tent that can't protect them from the blazing sun or the raging wildfires that destroy one country after another. Or wherever else those weaklings now weep and bow their heads.*

Not Iris.

With steady steps, she gets up from the floor and picks up the lump that used to be her phone. She runs her fingers over the cracked surface, almost admiring its damaged new form. Her chin set higher than before, Iris kicks off the steel-toed boots, then steps to the window and sits on the sill. Downstairs, a horse whinnies in its sleep. Iris sets the phone on the windowsill like it's a trophy—a reminder of the only person who refused to take a bow in this new, fucked-up world.

A reminder of the new Iris.

Powerful Iris.

Strong-willed Iris.

Winner Iris.

She pushes the wheelbarrow up the wooden plank, careful not to slip on the icy edge. At the top of the muck pile, she places her boot on the wheelbarrow's tire to keep it steady, then tilts it over to empty the manure down the pit. Then she backs up, turns around once back on solid ground, and starts pushing the wheelbarrow back up toward the barn.

The last few days, Iris has worked harder than she's ever worked before. Tina's on sick leave for a cold, or flu, or something else Iris doesn't really care about. Personally, she believes it's Tina's shattered, broken-down ego that made her sick, demanding its time to heal. Though Timothy hasn't announced his decision on who will ride for him at the Cup, Iris feels confident about her chances.

Because something has changed.

While Tina's on sick leave, Timothy's given the horses some time off too. With the exception of light lunging work, Iris hasn't trained any of the horses for two full days. He's also stopped yelling at Iris. Or better yet—he's stopped talking to her altogether. But it's not a sulking kind of silence. It's more like his mind is occupied. Too busy for conversation or the latest updates on Van Dijk's algorithm.

Iris takes it as a good sign. A new way of being. Their relationship is morphing, finding a calmer form so she can take over riding Alfred—and win them a luxury future right here in Iceland. Timothy's giving her a chance. She can tell. And just the fact that his overstepping his boundaries in the viewing room a few nights ago hasn't happened again proves Tina's warning about him wrong. Whatever those two used to have going on at the main house has nothing to do with Iris, or the working relationship she has with Timothy.

Humming a tune that's been stuck in her head since the morning, Iris pulls the wheelbarrow with her into the last uncleaned stall. She grabs the pitchfork and starts shuffling the wood shavings, separating the manure balls from the clean bedding. The sun streams through the stall's metal bars. It's about eleven o'clock in the morning, she gathers from the sun's position. That means she's an hour early with her chores.

Her humming changes to whistling as she piles more clean bedding into banks against the stall's wall. After picking out every poo and wet spot in the box, Iris pushes the wheelbarrow back to the aisle and starts spreading the clean bedding back across the stall floor. She now sings aloud, struggling to remember the words to the old jingle. Iris shakes her head at herself and gives a small laugh.

"What's so funny?"

His voice gives Iris a start, sending her spinning on her heels. Tim stands by the stall door, leaning against the chewed wooden frame, holding a metal flask. He takes a long gulp, then offers it to Iris, shaking the flask while raising his brows. "You want a drink?"

"I'm good," Iris says, her voice calm and collected. Her new confidence doesn't go unnoticed by Timothy. He runs his tongue over his lower lip and narrows his eyes at his working student. Iris gives him a quick smile, then returns to flatten out the bedding. "Won't do us much good if Tina's out cold because of flu and I'm drunk or hungover, unable to work."

"I bet you could be drunk out of your mind and still have this barn done in half the time that little wimp ever could." He stops to take another sip. When Iris glances over, she sees something predatory flashing in his eyes. How drunk is he, exactly?

"Have you thought about the Cup?" Timothy asks.

In a matter of a half-second, the sensation of a thousand daggers pushes away the alert restlessness that has taken over Iris's stomach. *That's all I ever think about,* Iris almost blurts out but doesn't. She gives the clean stall a final approving look, then turns to walk out to the aisle. But Timothy blocks her way, spreading his long arms on the stall's doorway, so the only way Iris could leave is ducking under his armpit. She takes a careful step back and forces herself to meet Timothy's drunken stare.

"What about the Cup?" she asks, this time with less confidence in her voice.

"You . . . " he says. He goes for another sip, but the way he ends up shaking the flask and grunting instead, tells Iris he's run out. "You riding Alfred, of course." He takes a step into the stall, then turns around and pulls the sliding door shut with one quick hand movement. The flask falls into the shavings.

Iris fights the urge to take a step back. She lifts her chin higher and takes a deep breath, forcing a small smile. "You know I want to ride Alfred in the Cup." She pauses to take a small step closer to the drunken man. "Just like you know I'm the one who will win the whole damn thing. Me—not Tina."

His chuckle is followed by an approving nod. One step, and he's standing right in front of Iris. He cups her chin, his fingertips digging painfully into her face. The smell of alcohol on his breath is nauseating. "How badly," he murmurs. "How badly you want it?"

"More . . . " Iris has to stop to force a sliver of air into her lungs. "More than anything."

"Yeah?" His fingers tighten. "Prove it."

Do whatever it takes, her inner voice rages at Iris as she's about to let her mind slip into the mental vessel and travel far away from this stall. *Whatever it takes to get your ass in that Cup. The old Iris would run and hide, like the coward she was. But not us. Whatever. It. Takes. I don't care if it kills you.*

Iris lifts her gaze and narrows her eyes. She focuses on her breath and the pain that Timothy's fingers cause. That pain feels good, she suddenly realizes. That pain is her new vessel, her way of tolerating whatever this world is to throw at her. She will take it. She will own it.

She will fucking survive.

"What do you want me to do?"

An owl hoots somewhere nearby. Iris sits against the open attic door in the highest part of the barn building. No one will find her here. For some reason she doesn't allow herself to think about, she doesn't want to sleep in her bedroom tonight. Not even with its door locked. She wraps the heavy-weight horse blanket tighter around her shivering body while the images from this morning flash through her mind.

Her knees landing on the wood shavings.

Her shaking hands, opening two buttons and a zipper.

His moans filling her ears.

Shaking her head, Iris gasps for air. *Doesn't matter now*, she tries to convince herself. *You did what you had to do. To make sure your future is secured.*

Even her inner voice agrees, never murmuring a word in contradiction. She's made it. In a month and a half, she'll ride Alfred in the World Cup. She knows the score she needs, the parts of the test that her strongest competitor will most likely not get right—the parts that she will excel at. She'll practice all day, all night. Give it all she's got. And once she's won, she'll come back home and no shitty corporation will ever be able to buy her freedom and force her to leave Iceland.

The images reappear, this time clearer, stronger, louder.

Her knees going numb as they dig through the shavings and meet the hard floor.

Her jaw throbbing.

Her eyes burning as she forces the tears back.

Pressing her face against the blanket, Iris screams into the horse-scented fabric. *No.* She will not let this morning ruin it for her. What's done is done. Timothy got what he wanted. Now it's her time. Anyone standing in her way will feel her rage and move aside while she claims everything she deserves, and then some. If she needs to deal with some fucked up flashbacks of this morning while she makes all her goals and dreams come true, so be it.

She can take it.

The *new* Iris can take it.

Sweeping the floor, Iris hears a loud groan and swearing from the viewing room. Tina freezes, half in and half out of the stall where she's been changing a horse from a rain sheet to a stall blanket. The wet sheet folded on her arm, she blinks a few times, turns to stare at Iris, raising her brows. Iris shakes her head at Tina, gesturing that she has no idea what's going on.

It's Tina's second day back at work, but Timothy hasn't said a word to her or Iris. No horses have been ridden, no training has taken place. Iris walks around like a shadow, doing her job but also trying her best to stay out of Timothy's way. Constantly alert and walking on egg shells, Iris and Tina both make themselves as invisible as possible. Though they've never been anywhere close to being friends—quite the opposite— these past few days, they work together seamlessly.

Tina closes the stall door and nods toward the grain room. Iris sweeps the dirt pile into the closest stall and closes the door. She follows Tina to the furthest room away from the viewing room. Once Iris is in, Tina peeks her head out, then lets the swinging door close behind her slowly. Iris sits on a stack of grain bags while Tina crosses her arms on her chest and leans against the wall.

"Okay," Tina half-whispers, "What the hell's going on with Walker? I mean, shitty mood aside, he's never given the horses more than two days off training. And a month before the Cup . . . Is he losing it?"

Iris crosses her legs and takes a deep breath before answering. She wants to deny there's anything wrong, but Tina's right. Even if Tim's decided to switch his top rider from Tina to Iris, someone needs to keep riding Alfred for him to be in top-notch shape for the World Cup.

"I mean, did he say something to you?" Tina continues when Iris doesn't answer. She stares at Iris intensely, narrowing her eyes. "Did something happen?"

Iris's head twitches as she blocks the mental images from entering. Before Tina can point out her involuntary tic; she hurries to say, "Nothing happened. He's just on a bender. People do that when they're under stress. I'm sure he'll snap out of it soon."

Tina keeps staring, investigating Iris's face. She's not buying it, Iris can tell. With a small pout on her full lips, Tina pushes her palm against the swinging door and peeks down the aisle, then lets the door swing shut again. "You slept with him. Didn't you?"

Iris can't help the gag reflex Tina's words bring her. Coughing, she bends over, then jumps down from the feed bags and circles the grain room, gasping for air.

"Are you fucking insane?" Tina hisses at her back. "You're, like, sixteen!"

Iris taps the faucet open and gulps water until the cold water calms her throat enough for her to speak. Eyes filled with rage, she turns to stare back at Tina. "Eighteen. And I did not sleep with him. Just because you like to whore your way to the top doesn't mean everyone does the same."

Two strides is all it takes for Tina to reach Iris. Her slap burns Iris's cheek, but she's too unprepared for it to dodge it—or slap back. Out of balance, she stumbles back and hits her lower back against the sink.

"I don't need this shit," Tina hisses, standing in the middle of the grain room. Even if Iris wanted to leave, she would have to pass her raging coworker, and something tells her that Tina wouldn't hesitate to slap her on the other cheek, then the first one again. "I was Tim's top girl when you were still in diapers learning to walk. Just because he's suddenly interested in scoring some Eskimo ass, doesn't mean it changes my status in any way."

Iris's head jerks back in surprise. A wave of calm travels through her as she stands tall and takes a step closer to Tina. "You might have ridden for Walker longer than I have, but that doesn't really make you anything special. One thing's for sure: you're clearly only rowing with one oar. Eskimos never lived in Iceland. Just like I never fucked Walker. If he's changed his mind about who's riding what and where, it's only because I'm five times better a rider than you ever were."

"Changed his . . . " Tina stops to grit her teeth. "Take that back, you fucking bitch."

Iris takes another step toward Tina, leaning in close enough to feel Tina's breath on her face. "Make me, *Kanar* asshole."

Staring each other down, they stand still with their fists clenched, neither willing to give in, but not attacking each other either. It's not until they hear Timothy's dressage boots stomping in the aisle that Tina takes a step back and drops her gaze.

"Tina?" Timothy yells, loud enough to make one of the horses outside whinny. "Where the fuck is my lunch?"

Tina hurries to the door, pushing it open. "In the house, Tim. I'll come with you." Before she leaves the grain room, she glances at Iris over her shoulder. "You think you're so fucking sly, don't you?" With a small smile on her face, she pushes the door wide open, keeping it from shutting with her boot. "I know what you did. I can tell, because he hasn't touched me for days."

"You've been . . . " Iris's voice cracks. She clears her throat to continue. "You've been sick."

Tina's laughter is dry and brief. "You keep telling yourself that. And hey . . . " She moves to the aisle, holding the door open as she turns to give Iris a nasty grin. "I hope you're not delusional enough to think that what you did is just a one-time thing."

Tina lets the door swing shut. As she follows Tim's footsteps out of the barn building, her yell echoes in the empty barn. "Have fun with that, Eskimo!"

Cracked and misshapen, the remains of Iris's phone reflect moonlight on the windowsill. One hand resting on her cheek, Iris stares at the phone, not wondering where in the world her mother might be right now, or how she's going to come up with this month's rent, but trying to get Tina's words out of her head.

She doesn't care about Tina's name-calling. She doesn't even care about the bitch-slap. All she worries about is that Timothy hasn't yet told Tina it would be Iris riding the stallion in the World Cup. Why hasn't he? What is he waiting for?

Iris closes her eyes, reliving the one ride she had with Alfred. The authentic connection she feels with the majestic animal was even stronger while she was riding him. She squeezes her eyes shut tighter and focuses on the memory of each movement they performed. Every turn she asks Alfred to take, every transition or tempi change, all she needs is to breathe. Alfred moves under her seat, strong and majestic, never missing a step. Like an iceberg providing shelter to Iris—and Iris alone—while the rest of the world drowns in its overflowing hate and greed. Gently, Iris closes her ring finger on the right rein and activates her core. The stallion holds back for half a second, then moves forward with circling, powerful energy, making Iris and him one. The tempo of his canter is steady, almost too slow, but he compensates for the lack of speed with the bounce and ease of his rhythm. Left stride, left stride, her mind's eye moves from Alfred's left ear to his right—all she needs for the stallion to switch the canter and perform a perfect lead change. Right stride, right stride—he does it again. Iris lowers her left hand for a quick scratch on the stallion's withers. He snorts, stretching his majestic neck an inch longer. At the corner of the arena, Iris sits heavier in the saddle and closes her left calf just behind the girth. The horse bends, shortening his swinging gait . . .

The knock on the door startles Iris into sitting up. Holding her breath, she reaches for the blanket and covers her body with it. For a moment, there's no sound at all. Iris gasps for air and loosens her grip on the blanket.

What are you, five? Go open the fucking door. The new Iris doesn't act this way.

Another knock on the door. Iris stares at the lock, wondering how much force it would really take for someone to just barge in through the raggedy door—locked or not.

"Iris? You in there?" Timothy's words slur while he raps his knuckles on the door for the third time. "We have some unfinished business."

Iris looks around the room, unsure what she's looking for or why. Without thinking about it, she strides over to the windowsill. She grabs the damaged phone, shoving it into her pajama pocket.

"Open up. I can hear you moving in there." The sound of stumbling and then Timothy cursing under his breath reaches Iris's ears. She forces herself to breathe, no matter how shallow the inhales. The room has started to spin slowly, and a strange buzzing sound starts somewhere in the back of her mind.

A fourth knock. "I want to talk about the Cup."

The buzz fades away. The room stops spinning. Iris takes a hasty step toward the door, every inch of her body spiked with excitement. She takes another step, then stops to hesitate. "What about the Cup?" she asks, her voice shaking more than she'd like.

"What do you think?" Timothy says and grunts. "You want to ride the damn stallion or not?"

Her feet act before she can think about it. With the memory of Alfred's canter swing filling Iris's body, she takes a few light steps toward the door and turns the lock. When she opens the door, the smell of alcohol slaps hard against her face—harder than Tina's palm ever did.

He's wasted. Drunker than Iris remembers ever seeing him. Leaning against Iris's bedroom door, the man looks at her for three seconds, then pushes past her, almost knocking her off her feet. She backs up against the wall, still clutching the door handle. Timothy looks around the room, grunting and chuckling to himself like he's enjoying some sort of an inside joke that Iris is not invited to be a part of.

"No pictures of mommy dearest?" he asks, plunging down on Iris's bed. He's not a heavy man, but the bed struggles under the impact. The corner of the bedsheet comes undone, now hanging loose by Timothy's leg.

"What good are pictures?" Iris says. *Oh, come on,* her inner voice snaps at her nervous tone of voice. *We can do this.* She remains by the door, still holding onto the handle. "I remember what she looks like just fine."

"Looks like you?" he asks and gives a brief laugh. "She small and feisty too?"

A throbbing, alarming sensation fills Iris's stomach. In the corner of her eye, she estimates the steps she'd need to take to reach the staircase leading down to the barn aisle—and outside. She calculates the meters between herself and the drunken man. Estimates Tim's intoxicated state and how much it would slow his mobility.

She could make it.

"I get it." Timothy sighs and waves Iris off. "I don't like to talk about my parents either. I mean, who does, right? They bring us into this world against our will. Then fuck us up while waiting for us to move the fuck out and make our own money. Just so we can buy them a spot in some shitty retirement home where they'll lie in their own shit while complaining about how their ungrateful children never visit their sorry asses."

Iris swallows, takes another breath. Should she run? Should she stay?

So he finally talks to you again, her inner voice says. *Offering you a spot in the sun. Just like you always wanted. And what does dainty little Iris do? She wants to run away like some useless coward. Just because he's drunk and venting about his parents doesn't mean that he's not telling you the truth about Alfred and the Cup.*

"Have you told Tina?" she asks, finally able to move, even if it's just to shift her weight from one foot to another.

"Told her about . . . " He stops to think, then snorts and laughs for a while before continuing. "Ah, I see. We're back talking shop. You really don't want to waste any time, do you? Not a fan of small talk?"

Iris shakes her head, the blue-and-white locks dancing around her face.

"Well, get your pretty little ass over here then." He pats the spot next to him on the bed. "Let's talk. And no more mumbo-jumbo sentimental bullshit, you're right. I'm sick of it. Less talk, more action. Am I right?"

Just inhale. Hold it. Exhale. The restless, throbbing sensation travels up to her midriff area. It travels all the way to her forehead, makes a U-turn, then swarms down her body, all the way to her toes. A sliver of air enters her lungs, just enough to keep her from passing out.

Breathe. Just fucking breathe. Don't you dare run off. Stand. Your. Ground.

"Um, hello?" Timothy says, his eyes suddenly sharper than before. Looking soberer, he waves his hand in the air to catch Iris's attention. "Where the fuck did you just go?"

"I'm here," Iris breathes, wondering whether it's Timothy or herself she's trying to convince. "I'm just…"

"A bit slow?" he says, all lightness and amusement vanished from his voice. He gets up from the bed, his gait less wobbly as he walks over to Iris. He places one hand against the wall next to Iris's head, and the other hand on her other side, pinning her against the wall. "You know," he says, his breath hot and smothering against Iris's face. "I always thought you were as dumb as a bucket. Mm, from the day I met you. But then again … " He brings his body closer to Iris, his hip now pressed against hers. "Buckets don't need to be Einstein to serve their purpose … "

The room spins around her, a full one-eighty. Iris escapes, not using her feet but her mind, entering her mental vessel, leaving her body. When Timothy turns her around, his rancid breath now huffing against the back of her neck, Iris is somewhere else entirely. Flying through the air, wind on her face. She closes her eyes, ignoring the harsh fingers digging into her waist. The sound of a dozen galloping hooves thumping against the ground fills her mind. Ignoring the groans against her ear, the slamming weight against her buttocks, she's safe in her mental vessel—her happy place.

Slowly gaining more and more distance from her body, still pushed against the wall, Iris steers the vessel to travel back in time. She floats over a small red barn with a herd of Icelandic horses and Shetland ponies running across a wintery lava field. She sees herself—a tinier, younger Iris—grabbing onto one of the ponies. Her short legs wrapped around the pony's plump frame, she closes her little fists on the rough mane.

A jingling sound fills her ears—laughter. Her own. Tears of happiness—or maybe it's the wind—fill her eyes as the pony gallops through the lava field. Powdered snow rises from the ground around them as the herd continues full speed ahead. She's not afraid of falling. She's only afraid that this moment will at some point end. That she'll be forced back home where her stepfather lies amid oxygen tanks in the living room, Iris's mother weeping hopelessly next to him. Iris laughs louder, squeezes her legs around the pony, telling her to gallop forward even faster than before. In this moment, nobody can catch her. Nobody can tell her she's supposed to cry because her father is dying—that *of course* she loves the man. He's her father, after all, his devotion and undivided admiration thicker than blood. Shaking her head, Iris laughs again, howling into the wind. The bad man would soon be gone. The bad man would never knock on her bedroom door again. Telling her she wouldn't be allowed to go to the barn ever again if she ever told her mother about these secret meetings in the night. The bad man would be gone—and little Iris would be safe again.

CHAPTER 5
THE SAFETY BELT
(5 YEARS EARLIER)

She wakes up from the cold floor, bundled into herself. Downstairs the horses are banging their empty feeders, demanding their morning grain and hay. Someone whinnies. Someone kicks the back of their stall, hard.

"Shit, shit, shit . . ."

Iris leaps up from the floor and winces as pain travels through her, the consequence of her too-sudden movement. She looks down toward her ankles where her pajama bottoms are bundled around the broken phone—the weapon she had picked up to defend herself but then never used.

Oh, like that would have solved it. You, smashing his skull in with a piece of plastic? It would hardly have killed him, just pissed him off more. It's over now. What's done is done. You opened the door, didn't murder your trainer, and guess what? Now you get to ride in the World Cup and win yourself a big fat paycheck that'll give you the freedom to do whatever the fuck you want.

Unconvinced, she steps out of the pajama pants, careful not to step on the phone's sharp edges. After pulling on clean clothes, Iris shakes her head and refocuses her thoughts on the day ahead. The chores. The schedule. That's what she needs to do. It's the only thing left to do. On autopilot, she would perform the same tasks in the exact same way as she does every single day. Just like always, she'll keep her mind too busy and her body too exhausted to focus on anything other than keeping the horses well-fed and shiny.

Another loud bang sends her toward the bedroom door. One of the mares is kicking the back wall of the stall, most likely causing the wood to splinter. Every day she's downstairs at five o'clock sharp to feed them. Every day—except today.

Ignoring the strangeness of her bedroom door being unlocked, she kicks her shoes on, then hurries toward the stairs and down to the grain room. One stack of buckets at a time, she loads the wheelbarrow and starts pushing it toward the back end of the aisle. A quick glance at the digital clock up on the wall tells her the harsh truth; she's an hour late. This has never happened before. The daily routine is ruined; the schedule is completely messed up. She should be tacking up Alfred for training, or at least getting him ready for another lunge line session in case Timothy skips the training again. Now, Alfred wouldn't have time to eat before exercising. This would get Timothy foaming at the mouth—pissing him off beyond belief.

Two sets of boot steps arrive at the barn. Light chattering reaches Iris's ears, making her move faster, dumping the buckets into the feeders as quickly as she can.

He hasn't told Tina about the Cup yet, she thinks. *No way would she be in such a chatty mood if he had.*

Timothy disappears into the viewing room. While Iris collects the empty buckets off the floor, Tina walks over to her, a small smirk on her face. Her shiny black boots stop at the wheelbarrow. "What's this, Mo?" she says, her voice filled with mockery. "An hour late for feeding?"

"Mind your own fucking business," Iris mumbles.

She places the two bucket towers into the wheelbarrow and rolls it back into the grain room. Ignoring Tina, who follows her in and then leans against the swinging door, Iris pops open the grain cans' steel lids and looks for the plastic scoop. It's nowhere to be seen.

"What's gotten into you, Mo? Someone piss on your popsicle?"

Iris looks up from the grain cans to frown at Tina. "Is that an insult? Because that doesn't even make any sense." She turns and looks around the counter space, then under the sink.

"You off your meds or something?" Tina says in her chirpy voice.

Iris slams the cupboard door shut. "Where the fuck is that scoop . . ." she murmurs.

Tina takes a few steps, her shiny boots moving to the first grain can. She leans in, then lets the missing scoop swing side to side as it hangs from her fingers. "Looking for this?"

Iris takes a fast step forward, reaching for the scoop, but Tina hides it behind her back. Eyes filled with satisfaction, she lifts her chin and fails to suppress her smile. "Why are you an hour late on the schedule?"

Iris narrows her eyes at Tina, then takes a step back. She reaches for an empty grain bucket from the wheelbarrow and leans over the tin barrow with it. Using her hand as a scoop, she starts tossing in the granola pellets.

"Polar bear got your tongue?"

Iris lets the small bucket fall into the can. She leans against the metal edge and hangs her head. Then she lifts her gaze to stare at Tina. Her rage doesn't go unnoted; Tina jerks her head back in surprise.

"I said . . ." Iris says, gritting her teeth. "Mind your *fucking* business."

It takes Tina a few seconds to snap out of her surprise, but soon, the usual smirk returns to her face. She tosses her long brown hair back and walks to the swinging door. "But you see, my dearest Mo. I *am* minding my business." She grins, showing her perfect row of white teeth. "Because you're supposed to be tacking up Alfred for me. Tacking, not preparing grain."

It's Iris's turn to be surprised. *No*, she thinks to herself. *No, she's making it up.*

"What?" is all Iris can say.

"Al-fred," Tina pronounces the word slowly. "The stallion I'm riding in the World Cup. Tack. Him. Up."

Swallowing painfully, Iris parts her lips to ask the question burning in her mind. But the words get stuck in her throat.

"Seriously, Mo. You look like a fucking blow-up doll."

"Did you talk to Tim?" Iris finally breathes out. "About Alfred?"

Tina frowns at her, then scoffs and heads to leave. "Yeah. He said the stallion just needed a few days to recover from the training. Something about an algorithm telling him so, or whatever. I can't really bother with that geek stuff."

"No . . ." Iris says, suddenly out of breath. "Did you talk to Tim about you riding in the Cup?"

Tina raises her brows. "Um . . . yes? I mean, that's *all* we ever talk about."

Iris closes her eyes, then clenches her fists. Without opening her eyes, she asks, "When's the last time you spoke about it?"

"What, the Cup? Just now, while walking over from the main house. We were going over the tempis, and decided to start with threes and go from there. Then leave the changes be for a while and focus on the canter pirouettes. I told Tim that's my strong point, and he said—and I agree—that we should still . . . um, hello?"

Iris marches past Tina, a loud sound ringing sound in her ears. Her whole face burns. Her blood seems to be surging around in her veins with not enough space to move. Her whole body is about to burst.

"Hey, I'm still talking to you!"

But she can hardly hear Tina's complaint. She stomps over to the viewing room, slams the door open, and walks right in front of Timothy, who's taking careful sips of coffee at the table, staring into numbers on Iris's laptop.

"You need to tell her," Iris says between her teeth. "You need to tell her right now."

Timothy stares at Iris with a disinterested look on his face. Without looking away, he brings the coffee cup to his lips and blows on it. After another careful sip, he looks back at the laptop and places the cup next to the computer. "Tell her what, exactly?" he murmurs without looking at Iris.

"That I'm riding Alfred in the Cup."

"Um . . . *Excuse* me?" Tina's squeal hurts Iris's ears. She's followed Iris to the viewing room, but Iris doesn't turn around to look at her.

Tim leans closer to the screen, then tilts his head as he reads Iris's notes on Van Dijk's latest algorithm calculations. "Huh," he says happily, then leans back and reaches for the coffee cup again.

Iris rushes over and slams the laptop lid shut. Timothy blinks a few times, then sits back and looks up at Iris, this time with annoyance in his reddish eyes. They stare at one another for a moment, Iris's heart bouncing against her chest.

"Tina," Timothy finally breaks the tense silence. He keeps his gaze locked on Iris's enraged eyes. "Go tack up Alfred. Warm-up time, ten minutes per side. Shoulder in, straight, counter-bend. Repeat. Just like we talked about."

Without a word, Tina walks over to the row of bridles and grabs the one under Alfred's name tag. Spinning around on her heels, she heads to the saddle racks and lifts the dressage saddle up to rest against her hip. With agitated steps, she leaves the room.

I'm going to faint, Iris thinks, but keeps her gaze on Timothy's puffy eyes. *I need to breathe. Or I'm going to faint.*

Timothy smacks his lips together, dropping his gaze. As if Iris never existed, he reaches for the laptop and opens the lid back up. The computer hums back to life. Iris acts before she has time to think. She swipes at the lid again, closing it, then picks up the computer from the table. Hugging it against her stomach, she fills her lungs with air so she can speak.

"You said it'd be me. That all I needed was to prove myself to you. Prove that I'd do anything to ride in the Cup. And you and I both know, that's exactly what I did." Iris pauses to let Timothy speak. When all he does is stare back at her, she repeats, "You *said* it'd be me."

"Yeah, well . . . " Timothy empties the rest of the coffee with one big gulp. He picks up an apple from the bowl on the table, gets up, and steps around Iris. "Now I'm saying it'll be Tina."

Iris turns to look at Timothy's back as he's about to leave the room. "Why?"

He freezes by the door. "Why?" he imitates Iris's voice, mocking her. He turns around to look at her with a look of loathing. "*Why*, she asks?" he takes two strides closer, leans in, and hisses at Iris. "Because . . . I

… fucking … *said* so. That's why. It's my fucking barn. My fucking horse. My fucking decision."

Iris holds her breath, something dark washing over her. It's hard to see. It's hard to hear. It's hard to feel anything but the strangling need to attack this man—this filthy, sick scumbag—and slam his head against the floor until he stops moving.

But when Timothy backs off to stand up straight again, Iris is frozen in place. The rage has paralyzed her. The pain from last night has turned from a throbbing nag into screaming, engulfing flames.

"Ah, good," Timothy says cheerfully as he peers out the open door. "She's already in the arena, warming up. See, this is how a proper student works. This is how it should be. Tina humbly takes an order, does as she's fucking told, and keeps her whining to herself." He tosses the apple in the air, then catches it and takes a bite. His mouth full, he points in the direction of the grain room. "Speaking of. Don't you have some chores to catch up on? Or are you just going to fuck off all day? Huh? Let me and Tina do all the work, as usual?"

Iris's whole body has started to shake. She stares at a piece of dirt, fallen from the bottom of Timothy's boot onto the viewing room floor, unable to move. Shaky breaths are all she manages. Shaky breaths—so she won't pass out.

"Suit yourself," Timothy says and leaves the doorway, taking another bite of the apple. The crunching sound seems deafening in Iris's ears. "This is why you'll never make it, Iris," he hollers as he leaves the barn aisle and enters the arena. "You're too hysterical. Too fucking weak."

The viewing room lurches and spins around her. The room changes, sounding like it's started to slowly sink toward the bottom of the ocean. Muffled hoof steps, as Alfred trots past the viewing room window. Timothy's uncharacteristically cheerful voice mixes with the thumping, followed by Tina's jingling, happy laughter. Her back against the window, Iris keeps staring at the dirt on the floor.

You're seriously going to let him walk away? her inner voice circles around her, whispering into Iris's left ear, then right, while it swims around her, radiating scorn and judgment. This is the first time she notices how the voice sounds more like her mother's than her own. *This sick fuck used you. He let you think that you'd get everything you ever wanted if you just played along like a good girl . . . How naïve can you be? How fucking pathetic? You let him screw you over—literally—and now you're letting him walk away?*

Her feet move before Iris knows what she's about to do. She marches into the arena and opens her laptop. She fills her lungs with air, then yells as hard as she can while she lifts her knee and bashes the laptop against it—smashing it in half. Once the pieces fall onto the arena floor, she stomps on them, her gaze locked on Timothy, who's standing next to Alfred and Tina in the middle of the arena—his filthy hand frozen on Tina's upper thigh.

"What the . . . " Timothy starts, but he doesn't have time to finish his sentence.

Iris whistles once, nodding at Alfred. "Alfred! Up!"

The stallion snorts and takes half a step back. He rears up on his hind legs without warning, kicking his front legs high in the air. Unprepared for the unusual and sudden movement, Tina falls back and lands on the footing with a scream. When Timothy rushes over to Tina and kneels down to check on her, Iris whistles again. Alfred lands down on all fours, snorts once more, and lifts his head up to look at Iris. He picks up a canter, heading right toward Iris. Without stopping, he passes Iris, slowing down just enough for her to run, jump up, and climb into the saddle, her hands grabbing onto his mane.

Without looking back or hearing what the angry voice yells after her, Iris wraps her legs around the stallion and leans over his neck. They gallop down the barnyard, onto the driveway, and off to the lava fields. The wind in her hair, she holds on tight. She isn't afraid of falling. With the enormous power accelerating under her as Alfred flies across the field, she refuses to enter her mental vessel. She refuses to acknowledge the burning tears in her eyes. She lets the pain radiate around her body until it numbs down into a throb. When the mental images arrive, mocking and cutting her, she doesn't shy away.

Her bedroom door opening in the dark.

Breeches covered with sawdust.

Pajama pants wrapped around a broken phone.

She keeps the images in her mind's eye—welcoming them—until they seem unreal. Slowly, they start drifting away.

In this moment, as Alfred's hooves thump against the hard ground and the silent field basks in the morning sun, she lets herself remember her stepfather's waxy face. Her mother's evasive eyes. Little Iris's bedroom door handle, slowly moving down in the night light's dim glow.

Unlike her mother, she dodges nothing now. She accepts what's happened. What they made her do. What she's become. For the first time ever, here on the galloping stallion's back, Iris lets the demons enter her happy place.

Let them.

Huffing, his neck covered in sweat, Alfred slows to a walk. Iris looks up from his mane, momentarily startled when she realizes she's lost all sense of time and place. His hooves clopping against the tarmac, Alfred heads up a well-groomed lawn and toward a water fountain—and a familiar hotel front.

By the front door, Iris pulls gently on Alfred's reins, coming to a halt. She looks around the silent hotel yard. Not a single vehicle is parked in the designated slots. Not a single guest wobbles past them, drunk or high on the new pills her mother used to rage about. At the resort, it's rare to see anyone sober these days, no matter how early in the morning. But no one's here at all—just Iris and Alfred.

She leans forward to swing her right leg over to the left, then slides slowly down from the saddle. Clicking her tongue, she asks Alfred to follow her to the resort's courtyard. The horses in there whinny and nicker, watching the strange approaching horse with interest in their eyes. Iris spots an empty but bedded stall at the farther side of the horseshoe-shaped yard. Without thinking, she leads Alfred in, takes off his saddle and bridle, closes the door, and throws in a flake of hay from an open bale nearby. Carrying the saddle and bridle, she enters what looks like a combined grain and tack room. In the corner, she spots a few western saddles on a rack and bitless bridles hanging next to them on the wall. She places Alfred's saddle on top of the less dusty saddle and hangs the double bridle on top of the bitless one on the wall.

The tack room has another entryway that leads straight to the hotel's front door. Iris wipes her hands on the back of her jeans and looks around. Still no one here. The yard is empty and silent, as if the resort has turned into a ghost town since Iris's dinner with her mother not too long ago.

"Why am I here?" she half-whispers. "What the hell am I doing?"

Unsure whether she's talking to herself or her inner voice—or whether they're one and the same—Iris stands still and listens. She waits for a snarky answer or a reminder of how idiotic and useless she is. How all the bad things that have happened to her are because she didn't make better decisions. How she needs to grow up and learn how to take better care of herself.

She hears nothing. Not around the resort, not inside her head.

She's all alone. And for the first time since she can remember—that's okay. It doesn't matter where she goes, why she's here, what happens next. She's alone, not because everyone has abandoned her— but because she wants to be. She's broken free from a mental prison her inner voice once created for her. And now, the voice has gone silent.

She walks to the hotel's front door, assuming it to be locked and sealed. Out of business, as nearly everyone in Iceland has now been relocated or retired to a land far, far away.

Cowards, she thinks and tugs on the door. It opens with a click.

Inside the lobby, the house plant sits by itself in the corner. Iris's steps echo in the empty hall. No lights are on, and not a single sound reaches her ears. She looks down the corridor, then at the restaurant, the bar.

Nothing.

Turning in place, Iris takes in the peace and calm. No clocks tick on the walls, no digital screens tell her how late or ahead of time she is on her chores. No tapping boots, no demanding looks. It's just her and an empty hotel in the middle of a country that everyone else has given up on.

For a reason she can't quite understand, she steps over to the plant. Kneeling down, she reaches for the soil inside, fumbling around until her hand touches something solid.

A martini glass.

She turns to stare at the door with the double-lock. It's cracked open, a brick shoved between the door and its frame. A dim yellow light glows inside. Warm. Inviting.

How did I miss that when I walked in?

Holding the martini glass, Iris steps over to the door. Leaning in, she listens. A low humming sound is all she hears, coming all the way down from what she believes to be a basement. With steady hands, she opens the door a bit wider so she can slip in. The tile stairs ahead look odd. They're made of some high-tech material Iris isn't familiar with.

Walking down the stairs, in addition to the machine-like humming sound, she hears a woman's voice. When Iris steps on the floor at the end of the stairs, a yellow tile lights up underneath her foot. In the middle of the room, Laura Solomon paces around in small, unhurried circles, her hands folded behind her lab coat, and a set of AR or VR glasses on her head. Nodding, she listens to whoever is on the other line, saying "yes" or "no" as her assured steps move her around seven strange-looking pods, standing upright in the room.

Blinking in the light from the tile, Iris tries to see around her. The basement is huge, it seems. The way sound travels around makes it seem endless. Narrowing her eyes to see further down the room, Iris stares at a row of silhouettes in the distance. Like tall buildings, they stand and hum steadily. She looks at the capsules next to Laura, then into the distance again. *What the hell is this?*

"Welcome back." Laura's voice forces Iris to look away from the rows and into the doctor's mesmerizing eyes, partly covered by the glasses as she lifts them with one hand to see past them. "Is that my martini glass?"

Her mouth gaping, Iris looks at the glass in her hands, then at Laura, then at the capsules in the distance.

"Are those . . . *people* inside?"

Laura lifts her index finger to indicate that she needs a moment. Placing the AR-glasses back on, Laura says, "What was that? What, no. No one's here. No, mother, listen. Just tell Nurse Saarinen to take in as many as she can. I have to go. Mm. See you tomorrow . . . That's what I said, isn't it? Tomorrow. Mhm, yes. I'll actually come home this time. I've got to go." She takes the glasses off and puts them on an operating table next to one of the capsules, staring at them in frustration. After a moment of deep, even breaths, Laura stands tall again and remembers Iris in the room. With the same assured gait as before, Laura walks over and reaches for the martini glass in Iris's hands. She wipes off a layer of soil and blows into the glass. "I was wondering where I left that."

Iris keeps her gaze on the rows of capsules in the distance. As though Laura hadn't spoken, she takes a few steps closer, hoping that the tiles that light underneath her muddy shoes will provide a better view. She walks over to where the rows start, steps up on a lifted base, and presses her face against the capsule's frosted glass. Inside she sees a sleeping but sickly and pale-looking woman. Mesmerized, Iris doesn't turn around when she hears Laura's steps approaching right behind her. "Is she dead?" Iris asks without taking her gaze off the pale woman.

"No."

"Is she sick?"

"In some ways . . . yes."

"Is she in a coma?"

Laura's coat fabric rustles lightly as she shrugs a shoulder. "In stasis. Has been for a few months now."

"But why?" Iris half-whispers, trying to tear her gaze from the sleeping woman.

Laura pauses, turns around, and steps on the stasis capsule's base. Her gaze locked on the martini glass in her hands, she turns around and leans her back against the capsule, raising the glass against the dim light from the staircase ahead. She blows into the glass again then looks at Iris, investigating her face like it's some sort of a puzzle.

"Well, let's see," she says and nods at a small computer pad attached to the stasis capsule she's leaning on. "Go on. It's easy enough to use. Has to be. I'm a doctor of western medicine, not computer science."

Without hesitating, Iris reaches for the pad and taps a button on its side. Another tap on the screen opens a control panel and an easy-to-read database. As she investigates the gadget, she waits for her inner voice to appear, scolding her for being this reckless and stupid. Doctor Solomon is a maniac. A madwoman with an underground graveyard for naked kidnap victims in the middle of the most public place in Iceland.

But the voice says nothing.

For the first time since Iris can remember, she feels safe. In the middle of this strange basement room, with a woman who's known for her megalomaniacal ways, a newfound assurance fills her mind. Down here, no one can harm her. In Laura Solomon's secret underground space, she's untouchable.

"You can read it?" Laura asks, nodding at the pad in Iris's hands.

"Yes," Iris says and nods back.

"I don't remember them by heart," Laura says, stepping down from the base. A yellow tile lights up under her white shoes. "But let me guess . . ." She turns to look at the capsule, tilting her head. "Postpartum psychosis leading to maternal filicide."

Iris taps open a folder under *diagnosis* and reads aloud, "A thirty-five-year-old female with chronic anxiety was brought in after a maternal filicide that took place in Vantaa, Finland, 2084. The patient was referred for further medical investigation and diagnosed with schizophrenia by a psychiatrist at Helsinki Universal Hospital. During her stay in the Finnish Mental Institution, she reported chronic pain in her lower stomach. The patient said she believed the pain to be a result of electromagnetic impulses sent to her ovaries via an electrical implant in her body. According to the patient, this device had been planted into her body two years earlier by a government organization . . . "

"Ah," Laura says, interrupting Iris. "I remember her now. And I was wrong; it's been longer than a few months for this one. She's one of the first ones they signed over to me."

Iris looks up from the pad. "Who did?"

"The Finnish government." Laura shoves the martini glass into her coat pocket. "Before they bailed out and retired. Cowards."

"I don't . . . " Iris shifts her weight, more intrigued than nervous. She's thrilled to learn that Laura seems to feel the same way about people abandoning their home country just as it needs them the most. That they're pathetic cowards. Though not everything the doctor is saying makes sense to her. "I don't get it. Finland doesn't have a government anymore?"

Her smile is not petty, nor is it friendly. "Would you be surprised if I said that Iceland doesn't, either?"

"Not really," Iris says slowly. "Not many people left to govern around here... But wait, why is this woman here in Iceland if she was first treated in Finland?"

"My dear mother," Laura says and pats the martini glass in her pocket, "said I need to use some of my mandatory vacation days. The company uses this resort every now and then for team building, meetings, that sort of nonsense. So I promised to come here and try out drinking and hotel life. But I never said anything about not bringing in some light work with me." She nods at the capsule where the woman rests in stasis. "I had a batch of long-term patients shipped in a few days before I arrived. And when the hotel refused to rent out the whole basement," she pauses to shrug, "I bought the place."

"You bought the whole hotel?" Iris says.

"No." Another shrug. "I bought Iceland."

A nervous laugh escapes Iris's lips. But as she stares at Laura, waiting for the woman to burst out laughing, too, then she realizes she won't. Doctor Solomon is not joking—she's actually somehow managed to purchase Iris's home country. "Is that why we have no government left?"

"Ah, no dear. I just quickened its end. Don't feel bad; it's the same all around. This is hardly the only country I've added to my cart as of late."

Iris sucks her lower lip in, unsure of what to say. She knows things are not exactly safe out there in the world. She knew that even before the media stopped reporting news from foreign countries. And she read about the mass murders on the internet. She knew about people dying due to untreated disease or by their own hand. But somehow, she thought it'd all work itself out. It always has before . . . eventually. All she ever needed to do was turn off the news and wait.

"How did she enter the capsule?" Iris finally asks, her gaze shifting between the sleeping woman and the pad in her hands. "Are you waking her up soon?"

"Well . . . " Laura walks back to the pod and tilts her head to investigate the woman inside, though she can barely see through the frosted glass. "That's the reason I remember her. Yes, she was brought to me by the Finnish Mental Institution as a lost cause. But I didn't have to use force to get her in stasis. She volunteered."

"She did?"

"Mm." Laura turns on her heels and heads back toward the operating table. She fishes the martini glass from her pocket and sets it next to a strange-looking helmet with wires poking out. "As soon as she learned that Pharma Salonen had nothing to do with our government." She runs her finger on one of the helmet's wires. "That our foundation's main purpose is to help and heal people . . ." A shrug of her shoulder. Laura turns around and gives Iris a matter-of- fact kind of smile. "She couldn't jump into that capsule fast enough."

Iris places the pad back in its slot on the stasis capsule and follows Laura over to the operating table. A tickling, vibrating sensation takes over her skin. She looks at Solomon with fresh eyes, her breath steady and calm.

Maybe she's not a megalomaniac after all, she thinks. *Maybe she* is *pure genius.*

"Are they all schizophrenic?"

Laura shakes her head once. "Not all. But some."

"How long do they stay in stasis?"

"As long as it takes to cure them."

Iris breathes in, excitement and wonder filling her. "How many capsules do you have?"

"Not enough." Laura grabs the martini glass from the operating table and starts walking toward the glowing yellow staircase. "You need a drink? The staff left for City of Finland this morning, but I'm sure I can manage to mix us something nice. Or if not nice, something drinkable enough."

Iris hurries after the woman. Once they're half-way up the stairs, she hears her own calm voice say, "Actually, I don't drink." She hopes this won't upset or disappoint Laura.

Laura looks over her shoulder at Iris, a half-smile on her face. Upstairs, instead of taking a left to head to the bar or restaurant, Laura turns right and pushes through the hotel's front door. Outside, she stops in the middle of the driveway and tosses the martini glass on the lawn. "Good," she says and gazes up toward the sunny clouds. "Me neither."

A horse whinnies at the barn, then two others answer until they all call out together, with one banging its front hoof against the stall door. Laura seems oblivious to the sound. Her face turned up toward the sun, she seems to be lost in a moment, stuck in the here and now.

Iris turns toward the barnyard, remembering Alfred and the reason why she's here in the first place. "The staff," she says, staring toward the sound of hungry horses. "You said everyone left this morning?"

"Mm. Not much to do here right now."

"Here at the resort?"

"Here as in Iceland." Laura turns to look at Iris, a small twinkle in her eye. "I bought the place, remember? And running a hotel or a restaurant is a tad below my pay grade."

When a loud bang sounds from the barn, Iris can't help it. She enters the grain room and then the court-yard where the horses nicker at her with enthusiasm. Iris goes around, tossing hay flakes over the stall doors. She feeds Alfred last and stops to investigate the stallion as he lowers his head to munch on his delayed lunch.

"I don't remember seeing a white one," Laura says from somewhere nearby.

"A gray," Iris corrects her. When Laura doesn't answer, Iris looks at the woman and gestures at Alfred's body. "The white horses are called grays. And you wouldn't remember him. He's brand new. I brought him in with me."

"Huh."

"What are you going to do with the horses?" Iris asks. "With no staff around?"

"Huh," Laura repeats. She looks around for a while, thinking, then shrugs her shoulder. "Can't say that I've thought about it." She pauses to think. "Can I just leave the stall doors open?"

"They'd run off."

Laura tilts her head at Iris. "Right. Problem solved."

"You want them to starve?"

This time she shakes her head, with a hint of surprise on her face. "Not at all." She looks around the barnyard, seemingly out of place. The animals aren't making her uncomfortable, but it's easy to see that Laura isn't used to being around them. "Just because they're an inconvenience doesn't mean I want them dead. You're saying they wouldn't make it? Out there free and on their own?"

Iris looks around the barnyard. She counts twenty horses here. Most look like chubby trail horses, probably used to entertain the tourists visiting the resort. "Without cars on the road or people . . . I suppose they could survive. But they will come back for food. Especially during the winter."

Laura nods a few times, staring at Alfred. After a moment of silence, she asks, "Suppose you haven't changed your mind? About that job?"

"I don't know . . . " Iris says, though a wave of relief rushes over her. "Is it still open? You said there's not much to do around here anymore."

"I did," she says. "But then you pointed out a flaw in my plan." Laura nods at Alfred.

"So I could work here? At the barn?"

"I guess that depends."

"On . . . ?"

"What's your salary request?"

"What are my chores?"

"Well . . . For now . . . " Laura nods again at Alfred. "Keep the horses alive and your eye on the hotel while

I'm gone. Later, we can figure it out. I mean." She gives Iris a quick smile. "*If* I can afford you."

Alfred stretches his neck to poke Iris on her cheek. Absently, Iris pats the horse's soft nose while she thinks about what to ask for salary. She needs this. So badly. She's out of money, homeless, yet unwilling to leave Iceland behind and move to who knows where to live at the mercy of some foreign government with foreign rules. "Room . . . " she says, still patting Alfred, "and board for my horse." She wonders if Laura notices her voice shaking when she lies about Alfred being hers.

Surprise washes over Laura's face. With crossed arms, she tilts her head slightly and investigates Iris's face. "Let me get this straight, dear. I just told you that I bought a *country* . . . And your answer is 'will work for food?'"

Iris sucks her lower lip in. "I guess I'll need food too. Yes."

Her laughter is genuine, not mocking. Laura shakes her head and walks over to Alfred. Keeping a safe distance, she looks at the horse, respect in her eyes. "You're not afraid to ride a seven hundred kilo animal with a will of its own. A beast that could kill you in a heartbeat. Yet the first opportunity I give you, you sell yourself short. *Way* too short." Laura shakes her head again. "How has this world not eaten you alive?"

It has, Iris thinks as she runs her hand on Alfred's muscled neck. *But I won't let that happen again.*

"Room, board, food . . ." she says, her voice steady. She turns to look straight into Laura's eyes. "And five hundred thousand a month."

Laura doesn't blink. "Dollars?" she asks. "Or Euros?"

Iris's heart skips a beat. She stares at the woman, trying to see a hint of humor in her expression. "Icelandic krona," she says slowly.

Laura laughs again. "Well, dear. It's a good thing I found you. Because once we get the cities going, a salary like that won't feed you for a day. Didn't you say you can code? Why haven't you taken a job with the big four?"

"I won't work for some shitty-ass corporation that makes money out of people's misery."

"Mm. But you'll work for someone who stores people in stasis capsules? Without knowing the what, where, and why?"

Iris narrows her eyes. "That's different. You're healing them."

Laura pauses to stare at Iris, hesitating, but only for a second. "What if I told you there's more to it? That, yes, I agree with my mother that people need help. But that some people's minds are simply too far gone—too sick—to deserve another chance. Murderers, sociopaths, serial killers, rapists . . . "

Iris winces at Laura's last word. She turns her gaze away, swallowing loudly. Her face flushes. Not because she's embarrassed, but because of the rage that has started to once again bubble at the bottom of her stomach.

You will not let that sick fuck ruin this for you. Laura Solomon will never find out how weak you've been. Not now, not ever.

Laura notices the change in her body language, Iris is sure. She waits for her to ask about it, or to give Iris some sort of motherly advice, or tell her that she's not the only one, so just snap out of it and move on. But move on somewhere else—because the great Laura Solomon can't stand weakness and damaged goods near her powerful self.

But Laura says nothing.

Alfred's muzzle finds Iris's hair. The stallion grooms the side of Iris's head, forcing Iris to step back to keep her balance. She takes a careful peek at Laura, wondering if she'll just walk away, not bothering to explain why Iris isn't good enough to work here after all. But the woman's face shows no emotion. Her gaze stays locked on Iris when she finally speaks again. "A room," Laura says slowly, "Board for your horse. Five hundred thousand

CCs a month. And one stasis capsule. That'll be your pay."

"CCs?"

"Chip-Currency. It's the latest and the last currency we'll ever use."

Iris frowns. Not because of the currency; she now remembers her mother paying for their last supper with it. No, her forehead wrinkles because of the doctor's offer. Could it be? She *is* going to hire her? And what—a stasis capsule? What is this? Is she in danger? Not a cell in her body tells her she will be. Not a single moment spent with Laura Solomon makes her feel as if she should be somewhere else. She feels safe. Trusted. Valued. And she hasn't even started to work for the woman yet.

"Why . . . What am I going to do with a stasis capsule?"

Laura gives her a quick smile. "Follow me."

Leaving the barnyard behind, Laura leads them to the back of the courtyard, where an open-ended hangar basks in the sunlight. Inside, Iris sees a row of vehicles. Laura steps to the closest van and presses her hand on the side of a pad similar to the one attached to the stasis capsules downstairs. The van's side door swooshes open. Rope, duct tape, shovels, plastic bags, shrink wrap, a heavy-duty trolly, and two strange-looking pistols cover the van's walls.

"What's all this?" Iris breathes, still scanning the inside of the van.

"An option," Laura says. She stands next to the van, her hands in her pockets. "A chance to gain back what was stolen from you."

"Stolen?"

"Mm."

Iris climbs in the van and kneels down to run her finger on the gun's smooth surface. At the end of the barrel, a sharp-looking dart points out. "No bullets . . . " she mumbles, then looks over her shoulder at Laura. "You won't . . . kill him?"

"Me?" Laura leans on the van and crosses her arms. "I'm not going to do a thing. This is for you. Part of your pay."

The strange, new calm Iris feels is unfamiliar, yet soothing and reassuring. Everything about Laura Solomon, this place, their weird exchanges, should feel wrong. Eerie. Terrifying. And yet, the only place Iris feels this comfortable is on a galloping horse's back. It's like she's finally come home.

"He'll come looking for Alfred," Iris says, running her finger on the other gun. This one has no dart at the end of the barrel. This one shoots to kill. "The stallion is worth millions of dollars. And I stole him."

"Good," Laura says, tapping the van's door, then gesturing for Iris to jump out. "Consider him a gift from Timothy Walker's new landlord. From me to you."

The hem of Laura's white doctor's coat flaps in the wind as she circles the van and opens the driver's side door. She jumps in, then leans over to push the passenger seat door open.

Iris blinks at her. "You know him?"

"What do you mean, do I know him?" Laura says, her voice not amused or annoyed. "I own this place. I know everyone who has refused to move away. I told you—just because they're inconvenient doesn't mean I'll erase them from existence. But I will keep an eye on them. I know their names, bank account numbers, criminal records, shoe sizes . . . " She shrugs. "Soon, I might know their thoughts and memories as well."

"And Tina?" Iris asks, surprised to realize she cares. "Are we shoving her in a capsule as well?"

"Tina can go home," Laura says. She presses her hand on the side of the van's steering wheel. The engine purrs to life. "I can have a jet take her back to City of Nebraska anytime. That's just one AR-call away."

Lightheaded, Iris gives a short chuckle. This is crazy. Everything she's saying is crazy. *Laura's* crazy. But that craziness eats away the darkness that has lived inside Iris for too long. It numbs down the pain from last night. Muffles the disappointment of missing her chance to ride at the World Cup.

Fuck the Cup, she thinks and climbs into the van. *Fuck riding for anyone but myself.*

"One more thing," Iris says while staring straight ahead, her head buzzing with adrenaline. "Once he's in that capsule downstairs . . . " She takes a deep breath, lifts her chin high. "I don't want him to ever see daylight again."

In the middle of the winding road, an old Chevy truck speeds toward the van. Powdered snow sprays from underneath the spiked tires. As soon as the driver notices the van in the distance, the truck accelerates.

"That him?" Laura asks with a calm voice. "Or Tina?"

Iris swallows. "It's him," she says, annoyed by the way her voice shakes again. "Tina doesn't know how to drive."

The calm she felt back at the resort is fading away. But at the same time, she feels more focused than ever. Like she did when riding Alfred for the first time. Every step counts. Not a second can be wasted. This is her chance to take back what Timothy stole from her.

Her dignity.

Her safety.

Her *soul*.

Laura takes her foot off the accelerator and lets the van come to a stop. Both hands on the steering wheel, she turns to look at Iris. A small smile on her face, she asks, "Ready to start making the world a safer place?"

Iris peers at Laura, but quickly turns back to stare at the approaching truck. She's scared. Terrified. But there's no way in hell she'll admit that to her new boss. Just like she'll die before letting Timothy know that he still holds any kind of power over her. It's only been hours since Iris stole the man's horse, zoned out, and found herself in the middle of an underground pod farm filled with unconscious people. Only hours—yet she's stronger than she's ever been in her life.

She opens the door and jumps out. Tapping her foot against the snowy road, she waits for Laura to circle the car and press her hand on the pad. The side door swooshes open. Iris jumps in and kneels to grab the stun pistol. Her hand wrapped around it, she freezes, her gaze locked on the other gun—the one with deadly bullets in it. Could she . . . Should she? She waits for her inner voice to give her the final push. To call her names, stomp her down, spit at her, telling her what a coward she is to even consider anything other than ending Timothy's miserable life.

But the inner voice is gone. It's not there anymore, no matter how deep Iris digs for it, longs for it, pleading for it to come out. The voice is not there—because she's become one with it.

Outside, a truck door slams shut, about ten meters away. Laura stands next to the van, her chest wide, face neutral, shoulders relaxed, her hands deep in her coat pockets. She leans her weight on her toes, then shifts to her heels and back again. She looks like she's in a line at a movie theater, waiting for her popcorn and soda pop.

"Who the fuck are you?" Timothy's voice booms through the air. It's immediately clear to Iris that he's been drinking heavily.

Laura looks at the man, her face still neutral. Then she leans forward again, shifting her weight on her toes, back to her heels, then toes again. Swaying. Waiting. The smallest smile twitches at the sides of her lips, but Iris is sure Timothy doesn't notice it.

"You fucking deaf or something?" His steps crunch against the snow. "Never mind." For a moment, no one says a word. Then Timothy's yell echoes around the van and the lava fields. "Iris! Come out of the fucking van, Iris!"

Her hand still wrapped around the stun pistol, Iris holds her breath.

"I saw your ass lurking in there. Didn't think you'd bump into anyone you know on your way to the airport, did you? Well guess what? You can tell your taxi driver to make a U-turn back to wherever the fuck you just came from. You're not stepping foot on that plane until you hand back what you stole."

Iris pulls the stun pistol from its slot on the van's wall, then reaches for the other gun, pulls it out as well. Kneeling, the van's passenger seat shielding Iris from Timothy's sight, she takes a deep breath, watching Laura in the middle of the road, her blond ponytail dancing in the wind. One hand in her pocket, Laura brings her other hand in front of her face to investigate a fingernail. She brings the nail to her mouth, blows on it, then shoves her hand back in her pocket. A sigh rises in her chest as she stares at Timothy with no emotion.

"Seriously? What the hell's your problem?" Timothy stomps over to Laura and stops a meter away from her. Iris stares at the man between the van's seats through the front window, knowing he can't see her inside the van. "Huh?" he keeps snapping at Laura. "You deaf *and* mute, too?"

Slowly, Laura's lips turn into a half-smile. She takes her hands out of her pockets, straightening the sleeves carefully. While Iris and Timothy both stare at her, she picks an invisible piece of lint from her spotless white coat. Then she crosses her arms on her chest and gives another sigh.

"I see. Just another dumb bucket of a woman then," Timothy says, snark in his voice. He steps closer to

Laura. "Not surprising, really. I mean, taxi driver is not exactly an occupation for the geniuses among us." He takes another step. "A bit cuckoo, too, are we? Light all burned out up in the attic?"

The last step takes him so close to Laura that if she were to lift her knee, it'd land bullseye on Timothy's crotch. If Timothy would look to his right, he would now see Iris pressing against the back of the passenger seat. But the man keeps glaring at Laura, clearly convinced that she'll soon give in and take a step back. But Laura doesn't move. She stares back at the man, that same half-smile lingering on her face.

"Though I got to say . . . " Timothy reaches out and places his hand on Laura's shoulder, "This specific dumb bucket happens to have a surprisingly hot body," his hand moves an inch lower, "for an older hag like you."

When Timothy's hand moves toward Laura's chest, the woman turns her face toward the van. Raising her brows, Laura seems to send some kind of a silent signal to Iris. Not out of fright or anger, either. If anything, Doctor Solomon seems amused, like she's a lion facing a tiny mouse that's threatening to take her life. But nothing about Timothy Walker's predatory ways amuses Iris.

A hot feeling swarming around in her stomach, Iris jumps out of the van, both guns pointing at her trainer's surprised face. The calm washes over her mind again. Her gait steady and light, Iris walks toward Timothy. Doctor Solomon hasn't moved an inch. When the man steps back from her, Laura lifts her arm to check the time on her watch.

"Hey, whoa," Timothy breathes out, chuckling nervously. "Easy there, tiger. You even know how to use . . ."

Iris lowers the stun pistol, lifts the other gun, and fires into the air.

"Jesus fucking Christ!" The gun's barrel points at Timothy's chest. Iris keeps walking as the man backs up to get away from her. "Iris, stop! Let's talk about this!"

Iris presses on, forcing Timothy back. "I think I'm all done talking." She tilts her head and gives him a quick, crooked smile. "But thanks."

"Okay, okay, okay." He tries to stop, stumbling on his own feet. He falls on his ass on the hard snowy road. "Let's just talk about this, okay?"

She stops right in front of his boots, looking down at him. After a pause, Iris shrugs, keeping the gun pointed at her trainer. "So talk. What do you have to say?"

The man raises his hand as if to block the gun that is pointed at his face. Out of breath, he squints his eyes at the bright sunlight behind Iris's back. "It was a misunderstanding. Okay? This morning. With Tina. I just needed some time to break the news to her."

"News?"

"Yeah. You riding Alfred. In the Cup. Of course it's going to be you. I mean," he pauses to give a small, nervous laugh, "we both know you're ten times the rider she is. Tina's got nothing on you. It's just . . ." He stops and huffs, changing elbows to support his weight and block the sunlight with his other hand. "See, Tina's unstable. Yeah, quite hysterical, actually. I took her in when her mother couldn't handle her crazy ass any longer. Drugs, I think it was. Pills and booze, rage attacks, self-harm. That sort of thing. Who knows where she would be if I hadn't stepped up and offered to take her in as a live-in working student."

"I don't. Care," Iris says between her teeth. "About any of that."

"Of course you care! You girls are friends, right? All those sneaky little meetings in the grain room . . ."

Iris takes a step closer, bumping Timothy's boot with her steel toe. She raises the gun to aim better. She's not much of a shot, but from this distance, it'd be hard to miss.

"Okay, okay, fine. Tina's a bitch. I'm an asshole. What can I say? You ride Alfred in the Cup. Okay? You ride him, make us fucking rich, and I'll send Tina back to America. Or no, better yet. We'll have Tina work in the barn, and you can live in the house, rent-free. We'll order a fucking chef to cook for us every day. Huh? What would you like, sushi? Because it's on the house!"

The gun doesn't shake. Her hand is so steady, Iris feels as if her body has frozen in its zen-like state. She stares at the man, listening to her body. No bubbling rage. No difficulty breathing. The anger she felt before is there, but now, it's not controlling her anymore. She's in control. Of her body. Of her mind.

"Come on, Iris," Timothy says, mistaking Iris's pause for hesitation. He sits up, wiping his hands together. "What more do you want me to say? What more *can* I say?"

Lips parted, Iris lowers the gun. She lowers her gaze and shakes her head once. "See, Tim. That's the thing . . . Or the problem." She looks up and lifts her chin. "I don't want you to say a damn thing. Not one word."

The stun pistol clicks as Iris aimlessly pulls the trigger. The dart lands next to Timothy's left shoulder. She's missed by half a meter.

"Fu-uck!" he yells frantically. "Aagh!" Scrambling, his back against the ground, Timothy starts spider-walking away from Iris. "You bitch. You fucking bitch. You can't do this to me. Don't you know who I . . ."

The second dart lands in the middle of Timothy's forehead. His whole body freezes. For a few seconds, he stares at Iris with bewildered eyes. Then he falls limp on the road, unmoving.

With the wind in her ears, Iris stares at the man. She feels nothing. No regret, no relief, no satisfaction. It's not until Laura parks the trolly next to Iris that she snaps out of her death stare.

"To answer his question," Laura says, her voice light with a hint of amusement. "Yes, I know who he is. He's test subject ICE25778." She pushes the trolly next to Timothy's unmoving body and gestures at his feet. "Grab the legs. Let's drag him over with the trolly. The van has an electric ramp." Laura moves over and grabs Timothy by the shoulders, murmuring, "This should make dear mother happy . . ."

Iris hurries to lift the man's legs. Slightly light-headed, she enjoys the adrenaline rushing in her veins. "Your mother?" she asks, just to ground herself in the craziness of this whole moment. "Why would this make her happy?"

Together, they drag Timothy sideways onto the trolly. Once Laura lets go, and Iris works on the trolly, slowly pulling it toward the van, Laura says, "In addition to drinks by the resort pool, she suggested I try exercising outside in the fresh air. Something about it being better for the mind than hormone and serotonin balancing."

Iris stops the trolly by the van. She leans in to look for a button to bring the ramp out.

"And I've got to say," Laura says while walking over and pressing her hand on the pad attached to the van's side. She taps in a command code, and the ramp pushes out from underneath. "I do feel kind of refreshed right now."

Iris can't help it; she bursts out laughing. Once the ramp has settled at ground level, she circles the trolly, then pushes on it, tilting it forward, so Timothy's sluggish body lands on the ramp. Laura taps in another command, and the ramp lifts up. Once it clicks into place, Iris and Laura roll Timothy's body in, put the ramp away, and close the door.

Even more lightheaded but still in a pleasant way, Iris calms down from her laughing attack. With a smile on her face, she follows Laura back into the van. The engine purrs to life. Iris sits in the passenger seat, buckles her safety belt, and looks at her new employer. A sigh of relief rolls off her lips.

"Now, are we ready?" Laura asks, both hands on the wheel.

"For what?" Iris asks. "To make the world a better place?"

The white coat ruffles faintly as Laura shrugs and gives Iris a small smile.

Iris meets her smile, then fixes her gaze on the horizon. "Ready!" she says, her voice loud and clear. "What do we do next?"

CHAPTER 6
CITY OF ENGLAND

Investigating her bleeding knuckles, Iris waits for the elevator to arrive. The Chip-Center is quiet, though it now has twice as many tenants since Owena, her friend—a man called Pickle—and the CFU leader Ef have moved in. Iris hasn't bothered to talk to any of them. Passing the weird six-year-old in the corridor, all she had for the girl was a stern nod. But to Iris's surprise, that's all the girl did as well; she nodded with Iris in sync, never stopping or saying a word.

Ef is here to gather troops to take down Nurse Saarinen. Together with Laura and those in the Egg, they're to come up with a strategy to stop the war that still rages in multiple AR-cities around the world. Together with City of Serbia, the United Inland, the black-market leaders, and the CFU, they are going to put an end to Nurse Saarinen's dictatorship.

Or that's what Iris has been told. The truth is, she doesn't really care. Not anymore.

Her chip is gone.

Her home country has been bombed to ruins.

The only person that ever took an interest in her, also gone.

She has no purpose in life. No one to push her forward, no one's approval to gain.

The elevator door slides open silently. Iris walks in and, as if on reflex, looks for her AR-glasses to give the machine an order to go down to the basement. But as soon as she taps on her pocket, a wave of disappointment washes over her. She turns and slams her hand against the bottom button next to the elevator door.

"Mediocre . . . " she murmurs. "Useless . . . "

Once the elevator door slides open again, Iris steps onto the glowing red basement floor. In the middle, a brighter light illuminates a row of operating tables, computers, screens, and other gadgets. Iris is familiar with all of them. She just can't search a database in her mind to use them. Not anymore.

In the distance between the smooth-surfaced, horizontal capsules glowing dimly with reflected red light, something moves in the dark. Iris reaches for her AR-glasses to zoom in, just to remember this is all the vision that is available to her.

"Shitty human senses . . ."

A man's silhouette appears between the capsule rows. A smaller shadow follows, marching determinately next to the man. Suddenly, a bark sounds from the basement's depths. Soon, a yellow dog jogs past the man and the child, heading straight to Iris with a tennis ball in his mouth.

"Wacko, stay!" Ef's voice booms in the space. But the dog keeps coming toward Iris, now leaping forward with excitement. He stops a meter away from Iris, drops the tennis ball, and wags his tail. When all Iris does is stare at the ball, the dog gives her a forceful bark.

"Sorry . . ." Ef says and stops by the dog, then kneels to scratch its neck. "He sure is cute and smart, but listening doesn't seem to come with the package."

Iris stares at the man with narrowed eyes. Owena stands between the man and Iris, scratching the back of her head and staring into space. Iris bends over to grab the tennis ball. She tosses it in the air and catches it, keeping her gaze locked on the excited dog.

"Wacko, sit," she says. The dog sits, licking its lips.

"Wacko, lie down." The dog does as he's told.

"Wacko, roll over." He rolls over, then sits again, alert and focused.

"Wacko, stay." Iris brings her hand back and throws the tennis ball deep into the basement. It clanks against a red pod somewhere in the hall. The dog sits still, his eyes locked with Iris's. "Okay, fetch," Iris says, sending the dog off like one of Nurse Saarinen's missiles. She stands up and crosses her arms on her chest, looking at Ef with a bored look on her face. "You were saying?"

The man gives Iris a grin. "Ah, yes. The dogs lived with you in Iceland. Totally slipped my mind."

"Why would you remember such a thing?" Iris asks listlessly. "You don't know a thing about me."

The man holds his breath for a moment before he exhales and crosses his arms, mirroring Iris's position. "I see. Just like little Owena here, you're not into sharing and fluffy, feely things. I can respect that. But you're still part of the team. And anyone in the team is important. So I do know a thing or two about you. And everything I've learned is," he pauses, "well, it's beyond impressive."

"Yeah?" Iris asks, no enthusiasm in her voice. "And which team is that? The Unchipped? The Chipped? The Chipped for the Unchipped?" She pauses to shrug. "Because I lost track a long time ago."

Wacko's claws click-clack against the tile floor. He drops the ball in front of Iris, then backs up and sits down, his gaze flickering between Iris and the fetched ball. Iris looks at Owena, then nods at the ball. "Aren't kids supposed to like balls and games?"

Owena snaps out of her thoughts. Her hand frozen on the back of her head, she looks at Iris with a serious look on her face. "Like cartoons and hopscotch?"

Iris frowns, opens her mouth to reply, but when none of the comebacks seem appropriate, she presses her lips into a thin line and looks at Ef. "What are you doing down here? The mother hen sent you?"

"No, she did not. Mrs. Salonen is resting. Gathering her strength for the meeting."

His words surprise Iris. For a second or two, she blinks and stares into space. Is the old woman not doing well? Is she sick? The thought hasn't even entered her mind until now. It would be much like Mrs. Salonen to hide her own discomfort or sickness to take care of someone else. And for the longest time, that someone else has been Iris, whether Iris herself liked it or not.

"No, it's curiosity that brought me down," Ef continues. "Checking out the famous London long-term storage pod farm," he says, craning his neck to look around the enormous, dimly lit space. "I knew it'd be ominous, but damn," he shakes his head, "I guess I didn't realize the immensity of it. Or how many levels deep this place goes."

Iris sucks her lower lip in, then forces her feet to move. "You've seen stasis capsules before," she says and heads straight to the operating tables to pick up a CS-key. After a few seconds of staring, she curses under her breath and starts tapping on the device, unable to access any folders or data through the database that was once her chip-mind integration. *This is going to take fucking forever.*

"I've seen plenty of stasis capsules, yes."

"So what's so different about this place?"

"No, you're right," Ef says. With his hands crossed behind his back, Ef walks over to where the red pod rows start. "It's all creepy as fuck. I guess it's just the way these bad boys look." He knocks on the top of the closest pod, "They look . . . *sealed*. As if they were never meant to be opened again in the first place."

Iris shrugs, opening a list under a heading called ICE. "Maybe they weren't," she mumbles.

Behind her back, Wacko barks again. Iris turns around to see Owena staring at the dog, then at the tennis ball, then at the dog again. Iris lowers the computer in her hands and takes a step toward Owena. "Just pick up the ball and toss it." The girl looks up at Iris, her round, enormous eyes blinking. "Pick," Iris says, her voice slightly softer. "And toss. Go on. You can do it."

Owena steps toward the ball, bends over to grab it, then brings her arm all the way back to toss it. Before she does, she looks over at Iris, almost as if to ask for a final okay.

"Just toss it. It's okay if it doesn't go fa . . ."

Owena throws the ball in the middle of Iris's sentence. It takes off with so much power, it looks like a machine of some sort launched it, not a six-year-old girl.

"Holy shit . . . " Iris says aloud.

"She might not have the chip anymore," Ef says, now standing across the operating table that Iris stands by. "But all that strength and knowledge is still with her."

Iris swallows, watching the small girl stand statically in place, waiting for the dog to come back. "Is she . . . " She clears her throat, her eyes locked on Owena's hand as it scratches the back of her head again. "Is she doing okay?"

"She's better now," Ef says while picking up one of the CS-keys from the table, flipping it around in his hands. "Better here with her friends than in some bunker with a murderous lunatic."

Iris frowns, now looking at Ef's face instead of at Owena. "When are your troops entering City of Spain?"

Surprise washes over Ef's face. His lip twitching, Iris is sure he's about to make a teasing comment like "Look who's finally back in business!" or "Oh, so you *do* want to do some actual work and not just to beat a stinky punching bag all day long?"

But he doesn't say anything. He even wipes off the smile and the surprise on his face. This makes Iris like the man a tiny bit more than she did before.

A moment later, he answers, "During the next outing. Owena here tells us Nurse Saarinen does leave the bunker occasionally, though not too often. The next time she does, we'll be ready."

"And that's it?" Iris says, snark in her voice. "Boom, the Nurse is dead. Everything is fixed. Life is good. Good conquers evil. No more mass murders or drugged up, mindless people giving each other one- or two-star ratings?"

"Quite the opposite," Ef says, smiling. He puts down the CS-key and looks at Iris with friendly eyes. "Once Nurse Saarinen is out of the equation, that's not the end but the beginning."

"Of what?"

"The real work. Rebuilding. Gaining trust. Healing."

A snicker escapes her lips, but Iris can't help but ask, "And how the fuck are we supposed to rebuild anything from this shit-storm? People are so far gone. Brainwashed. Weaker than they've ever been. As far as I know, they can barely wipe their own asses without taking a pill or looking up instructions on the AR-net."

Ef bursts out laughing. Wacko's bark fills the room as he returns to Owena, this time shoving the ball straight into the girl's hand. The faintest smile visits

Owena's face as she gets ready to throw the ball again, this time in a slightly less robotic manner.

"We've come up with a plan. A beta for a whole new program."

Iris crosses her arms on her chest. "A *new* program?"

"Mhm. The working name is the Freedom-Program. But we're still debating on that."

Another scoff. "You've got to be fucking kidding me."

"Nope, not kidding."

"This . . . " Iris pauses to circle her hand in the air. " . . . *program* of yours sounds awfully familiar to me. You're not worried about its . . . ethics?"

"Well, you know . . . Omelets, eggs, and such." His gait strong and military, Ef steps over to a stasis capsule, this one standing upright with a woman sleeping inside. Her long, black hair looks like a snake against her bare back. "We need to get people out of these capsules," Ef says, placing his wide palm against the tinted glass. "But how do we bring back hundreds of millions of people into a civilization that is killing itself off? We need peace. We need good people in charge, with a solid plan and a simple goal."

"Which is, what? To not get high on happiness-pills and simulated sex?"

Ef chuckles at her words. He turns and slaps his palms together, then nods at Iris. "That brings us to this time and place. It's time to go upstairs. We're having a strategy meeting with the Egg in twenty. I was hoping you would join. But it's totally, one hundred percent, up to you."

Iris stares at Ef's wide back as he makes his way to the elevator. He presses the button and starts whistling a tune Iris doesn't recognize. With the tennis ball in her hand, Owena joins him to wait for the lift. Wacko follows the little girl, then sits down behind her, his eyes on the ball.

Iris stares at the back of Owena's head.

Her chipless head, she thinks. *She's more powerful than I ever was. With more strength and data than my chip could hold in a lifetime. But she survived. She's still here, making the best of it. Still powerful. Still special.*

"Oh, I almost forgot." Ef takes a step to place himself between the elevator door and the frame to keep the door from sliding shut. Owena and Wacko step into the elevator, then turn around to stare back at Iris. "The Freedom-Program will have a test group. Some carefully selected people currently in stasis. We want to recreate the resort from Iceland, to use it as a base for the experiment. And I can't think of anyone who would be better suited to recreate the scenery and help William design the landscape than you."

After a pause, Iris puts the CS-key away and nods at Ef. "Doesn't mean that I'm coming to the meeting today?"

He lifts his hands in the air and gives her an approving nod. "Didn't say it did." He steps into the elevator and presses a button. "Just think about it, that's all I ask."

Just before the door slides shut, Iris clears her throat. "Wait!"

Owena reacts faster than anyone else. With a quick twist of her wrist, she tosses the tennis ball between the closing door and the doorframe. The door sensors locate the ball, sliding back open. With his mouth slightly open, Ef stares at the rolling tennis ball, then at Owena, then at Iris. "Um . . . yes?"

"This test group," Iris says, giving Owena an approving smile. "What are you going to do to them?"

Ef's lips press together. He frowns, his jaw moving from side to side as he considers his words. "What do you mean, do to them?"

"Are you keeping the test subjects as prisoners?"

"No," Ef says slowly, shaking his head once. "Not prisoners."

"Are they going to live in an AR-reality? In luxury?"

He clears his throat. "Not exactly. No." He pauses, hesitating. "We're going to run some experiments. We just need the situation with Nurse Saarinen under control first."

"Are you going to torture them?"

Ef's mouth opens, but not a word comes out. He glances at the little girl next to him. Owena lifts her gaze to look back. "Iris asked you a question, Mister Ef," she says. "It's rude not to answer."

"I wouldn't call it torture…" Ef says hesitantly. "No."

Ef takes a deep breath, holds it, then sighs in discomfort. "The test group will experience a certain level of discomfort, yes."

"Pain?"

Ef lifts his hand to rub the bridge of his nose. "Pain, yes."

"Emotional pain?"

"Yes."

"Physical pain?"

He drops his hand and gives a small sigh, dodging Iris's gaze.

"How is that somehow a more disturbing question for you?" Iris asks. "You really believe that emotional pain is any better than physical? Because if you do," Iris pauses to grit her teeth, "you're fucking delusional."

Ef spreads his hands as if to surrender. "Yes, Iris," he says. "The test subjects will momentarily be in physical pain during the experiment."

A tickling sensation starts from the bottom of Iris's stomach. She stops to consider what she's about to say, but only for a split second. Before she has more time to think, her feet take her to the elevator, where Ef, Owena, and Wacko step aside to give her room. She presses the button to the office floor, then stands staring straight ahead while the elevator door slides shut silently in front of her face.

"I'll come to today's strategy meeting. I'll help Bill recreate the Icelandic resort. I'll bust my ass down in the basement and sort out all the ICE test subjects in stasis and move them to long-term storage." She turns her head to look at Ef over her shoulder. "With one condition."

The man gives her a slow nod, frowning his brow slightly. "Which is?"

Iris gives him a half-smile, then turns to stare at the elevator door again. "When the time comes to get started . . . I get to add a person of my choosing to the test group. No questions asked."

THE END

Shoot! Book 14 of the Unchipped story is at a close. But don't worry, you can find out what happens next in Book 15 in the Unchipped series, DECHIPPED: THE DOWNLOAD!

My dearest reader,

You are simply amazing! Thank you so much for your support and readership! I can't tell you how much you reading this book means to me. I'm humbled and honored that you've dedicated your valuable time to experience the Unchipped universe with me. I'm still a newbie author, so if you were to leave me a review on the store you purchased this from, or Goodreads it would be a huge help! Short or long, doesn't matter. Reviews are the best way to help other readers find the Unchipped Series.

Want to stay in touch? I would love it if you'd subscribe to my newsletter:

@ www.TayaDeVere.com/HappinessProgram

You can also find me on:

Facebook........................@TayaDeVereAuthor

Instagram........................@TayaDeVere_Author

Goodreads........................@TayaDeVere

Bookbub........................@Taya-DeVere

Gratefully yours,
Taya

About the Author

Taya DeVere is a Finnish science fiction writer who loves telling stories about perfectly imperfect people in dystopian and postapocalyptic settings. Her characters are outsiders and rebels who stand up against injustice and form unlikely friendships with other rebels along the way. She is the writer of more than 21 books, and is always developing new stories to delight her readers. Taya's restless feet have taken her all over Finland, the United Kingdom, Spain, and North America. She lived in the United States for seven years but is currently based in Turku, Finland with her partner, Chris.

Best things in life: friends & family, memories made, and mistakes to learn from. Taya also loves licorice ice cream, secondhand clothes and things, bunny sneezes, salmiakki, and sauna.

Dislikes: clowns, the Muppets, Moomin trolls, dolls (especially porcelain dolls), human size mascots, and celery.

Taya's writing is inspired by the works of authors like Margaret Atwood, Peter Heller, Hugh Howey, and Blake Crouch.

Final Thanks

"The horse world broke me."

It wasn't me who said this on a social media post this week but a friend. And yet, her words scraped the surface of some profound, old scars of mine. And it did it with such force, I've been scratching my skin for days. Usually, I don't care to acknowledge these partly open wounds at all. Like the old tattoo on my back, I rather forget their existence. But just like that (damn ugly) tattoo of mine, these scars are still part of my skin. And I guess it's about time for me to admit their unwelcomed presence. Horse world. It can be a brutal place. Harsh. Calculative and nasty. Nine times out of ten, it ends up damaging your skin instead of making it thicker.

But just like every coin, the horse world has its flip slide. A beautiful, wonder-filled flip side. And it's not just the majestic, amazing animals one gets to work and live with, but people too. It's an encouraging bump on the shoulder after a good ride. It's a knowing smile when your horse refuses to meet you at the paddock's gate. A late-night text message asking if you're feeling okay after a trying day at the barn. It's caring, loving, fun people who genuinely want to see you succeed and be happy. During my ten-year equestrian career, I found a handful of these rare gems while sorting through the manure piles.

Thank you, Jackie, Sybille, Kate, and Sari, for your friendship and unwavering kindness. Being your friend makes the itchy scars worthwhile.